FADING BLUE

Roger Busby

Illustrations by John Whittaker

Police Review Publishing Co. Ltd.

14 St. Cross Street, London EC1N 8FE

ISBN 0 85164 012 5

Electronically typeset and printed by Heffers Printers Limited, Cambridge, England

CONTENTS

Page

1. The Inspection 5
2. S Division 9
3. The Inspection 34
4. The Arrow Bridge Jumper 36
5. The Inspection 56
6. Detectives 60
7. The Inspection 78
8. Bishop's Waistcoat 82
9. The Inspection 99
10. The First Police Astronaut 104
11. The Inspection 118
12. Psychic Squad 121
13. The Inspection 143
14. Crime Intelligence 150
15. The Inspection 166

Author's Note:

In view of my long association with the police service I believe something more than the usual disclaimer is called for. Characters, locations and events portrayed in this book are entirely fictional. No comparison should be drawn with real people or events either past or present. The story is for all my friends who, despite the trials and tribulations of 'the job' have never lost their sense of humour.

One The Inspection

A STAFF car flying the pennant reserved for ceremonial occasions was coming down the dual carriageway. The driver held the speed at an even 50 miles an hour. Police patrol cars were parked strategically in lay-bys along the route and as the limousine swept past, the crews busied themselves flipping the VASCAR on and off and talking enthusiastically into the radio. When the staff car had passed they returned to their crossword puzzles, paperbacks and cat-naps.

'Tell me Henry,' remarked Sir Ralph Hawk, comfortably at ease in the rear seat of the limousine. 'If you were looking for one quality in the PCs what would it be?'

Beside him in the back of the car which was divided from the driver by a glass partition, Henry Grey smoothed his toothbrush moustache with a forefinger before replying.

'Loyalty Sir Ralph,' he said finally. 'Yes loyalty.'

'Did I detect a moment's hesitation?'

'I would have said discipline – but times have changed.'

'And standards have slipped?'

Grey was careful how he answered. 'Not entirely sir. No – just that, well . . . the priorities have changed.'

'You regret that?'

'Sometimes I do. Yes, to be honest I do.'

Grey surprised himself with his own candour. Sir Ralph was a wily old bird, he thought to himself, and lulled by the easy familiarity in the cruising limousine he had succeeded in throwing him off his guard.

'On the other hand,' Grey added, anxious that his remark should not be misconstrued. 'I've got nothing against progress – we must move with the times Sir Ralph, no one appreciates that more than I do.'

'Quite so Henry,' Sir Ralph replied enigmatically. 'Quite so.'

Grey looked ahead through the partition, contemplating the back of the driver's head. Under the cap the hair was a little too long, verging on the untidy and the sight irritated him. Back when he had been a sergeant the PC would have been on report for neglecting his personal appearance, now that he was the Deputy Chief Constable he was powerless to do more than verbally reprimand the miscreant. Yes times had certainly changed. No pride in the job any more.

Sir Ralph Hawk, Her Majesty's Inspector of Constabulary understood, of that he was sure. Why in those days there were short back and sides all round on the eve of an HMI's visit and woe betide the PC whose boots and buttons weren't gleaming. Oh yes, Sir Ralph understood all right. Within police circles, the HMI's annual inspection tour of the force used to be regarded as akin to a Royal progress. Now it tended to be dismissed merely as a quaint custom. Time was when a chief constable would never have dreamed of delegating such an important event as the HMI's inspection to his deputy. But with the new breed of chiefs coming up it sometimes seemed as though all the old traditions of the service had flown out of the window.

A heavy silence fell in the rear of the staff car. Staring ahead, Grey glowered at the back of the driver's head. The HMI's itinerary had been published in Force Orders well in advance so that everyone knew what was expected of them. It was too bad that the young man hadn't had the common courtesy to get a haircut.

Stiff and starchy, Henry Grey sat rigidly in the rear seat beside the HMI. They were both long in the tooth, old soldiers who still hankered for the military life, the pomp and ceremonial of the regiment. Henry Grey in his immaculate uniform, starched white collar, brown leather gloves and silver- topped cane resting across his knees, could have been a throwback to Edwardian times. He even sported loops of silver chain across his tunic, an embellishment of dress uniform long since out of fashion. His face was scrubbed, his short hair immaculately barbered. Every inch an officer and a gentleman. Who would have guessed that at the pinnacle of his military service he had foot-slogged through chilling rain behind the tanks rolling through Normandy, a bedraggled infantryman with nothing more imposing than corporal's stripes on his arm.

'It's a poor substitute though,' said the HMI, breaking the silence.

'Sir?'

'Loyalty, Henry – it's a poor substitute for discipline.'

'Oh quite so Sir Ralph,' Grey agreed. He enjoyed accompanying the HMI, dressing up for the occasion and observing the niceties of etiquette. And as an added bonus he felt they had a lot in common. He smiled: 'If I had my way . . . . .' He left the remark unfinished and Sir Ralph Hawk raised a bushy eyebrow.

'Go on man.'

'It's presumptuous of me Sir Ralph.'

'Then let me finish it for you. You'd tighten up the other ranks, eh Henry, the creak of leather, the gleam of a polished toe cap. Don't be afraid to say it man.' He leaned forward and tapped Grey's knee in a confidential gesture. 'Too many liberties taken in the service these days. Now in my force . . .' Sir Ralph paused for reflection. He had been Chief Constable of one of the minor shires before his elevation to the Inspectorate and he had ruled his force with the iron discipline of a martinet '. . . in my force, discipline was the order of the day. Men knew where they were and respected you for it. How can you expect loyalty if you have to say please every time you want a job done. If I had *my* way, I'd put the clock back tomorrow.'

'Some of the youngsters coming in these days,' Grey said, 'they'd never have made the grade in my day. Sergeants and inspectors in their twenties, heads stuffed full of sociology.' He frowned his displeasure, 'In my day you had to get some time in before you earned your stripes.'

'Quite so,' said Sir Ralph Hawk. 'That's what I like about you Henry, we understand each other, bit of the old military backbone. Not many of us left.' Sir Ralph had spent his war soldiering behind a desk as a major in the military administration of the Rhine, requisitioning everything from tanks to toilet rolls. 'Tell me how'd you get on with your Chief?'

Henry Grey stiffened. 'Perfectly well sir – why do you ask?'

'Bit too much of a fresh-faced college boy for my liking. Still wet behind the ears.'

Grey stared ahead without commenting. Whatever else he might be, the Chief Constable was his superior and it went against the grain to criticise a superior, however laudable the motive.

'I imagine you don't exactly see eye to eye,' Sir Ralph pressed the point with a smile.

'Sir I'd rather not express an opinion, unless that's an order.'

Sir Ralph laughed. 'That's exactly what I expected you to say – know when to keep your own counsel. You're a good man Henry.' Then to ease Grey's discomfort, he abruptly changed the subject: 'So – what's the plan of campaign for today?'

'S Division sir,' said Grey thankfully. 'Take a look-see around the headquarters, warmer-upper in the mess and then a spot of lunch.'

'Capital,' Sir Ralph replied. 'Who's in charge of the division?'

'Cheep sir – Maxwell Cheep.'

'New man?'

'Yes sir – the S tends to be a bit of an outpost. The Chief sent Cheep out to lick 'em into shape.'

'Got it in him has he Henry?'

'He's loyal Sir Ralph,' Grey said.

He was staring at the driver's neck again. That man definitely needed a haircut. He'd take it up with the head of the Traffic Division.

'Cheep,' Sir Ralph Hawk rolled the word around his tongue, 'that's a damned funny name . . .'

Two S Division

MAXWELL CHEEP was a prize berk. Who said so? Just about everybody on the S Division from the panda jockeys and the beat Bobbies right up to Harry Curtiss, the deputy, who more or less had to run the division single-handed. According to the well-informed sources of the canteen mafia, Cheep had achieved his rank by licking boots and backsides. It was also claimed, mainly in CID circles where such matters were deeply pondered, that Cheep suffered a chronic hormone deficiency which had resulted in the majority of his hair falling out. This opinion was supported by the fact that the divisional commander wore an ill-fitting toupee which he would often tilt with a little finger to scratch his balding pate.

Cheep by name and 'cheap' by nature. As an embellishment to this irreverent suggestion someone came up with the risque story that Chief Superintendent Maxwell Arnold Cheep performed his daily exercise by puffing up a life-size inflatable rubber replica of Marilyn Monroe, seized in some obscure vice raid, which he would then proceed to ravish with gusto within the sanctity of the Divisional Commander's private bathroom. In the constant gleeful play on his surname, such activity was referred to as a 'Cheep thrill'.

Now on this particular morning, as Harry Curtiss made sure that the oak panelled conference room was prepared in fitting style for the divisional commander's weekly pep-talk to his senior ranks (Cheep called them his young lions which brought winces all round), seeing to it that the blotters were squared around the mirror polished table, that the pencils were sharpened just so, Cheep was also a stickler for irrelevant detail; the superintendent who had more time under his belt than he cared to recall reflected upon the former glories of the converted mansion which now served as the S Division headquarters.

As the others drifted in and took their places, Curtiss remembered times when the mansion had been the headquarters of the old Borough force, in those halcyon days before amalgamation, when the chief constable and his entourage held court in this very room; when the chief's spacious suite adjacent to the conference room housed the Borough's finest, not some cheap-skate (Curtiss groaned inwardly. . . even he was doing it now): Why in his heyday, when he had been staff officer to the chief himself, Curtiss alone had been permitted to operate the dumb waiter that whisked those confidential files from the chief's desk to sacred ground within the Administration Department without exposure to the prying eyes of civilian clerks who could never really be trusted. At least the dumb waiter remained as a memento of those past glories despite the atrocities of double glazing and wall-to-wall nylon carpeting which to his mind detracted from the dignity of the old house.

But times had changed and Curtiss was not one for harping on the past for long. When the old Borough force became the S Division of the new County Constabulary, Curtiss bounded from inspector, through the chief inspector rank to become deputy of the division. Career-wise the amalgamation had been good to him, but there were drawbacks, and the biggest was Maxwell Cheep. He had come from a desk at the County headquarters, a product of a system that tended to keep kicking its most useless elements upstairs in the fear that they might do some irreparable harm where they were. The system kicked Maxwell Cheep into the S Divisional Commander's chair, gave him five hundred policemen and a territorial area from a market town right down to the coast as his own domain. They said there were only two good jobs in a police force, chief constable and divisional commander, God and little God, each in his own way virtually autonomous.

Curtiss abandoned his reverie, and had them all seated and looking reasonably presentable when at the allotted time, on the stroke of ten-thirty, the door leading through to little God's chambers swung open and Maxwell Cheep entered the conference room. Strutted would have been a better description, for he had the bearing of a bantam cock, a small man barely making the height requirement, chest thrust out with his own importance, eyes flinty in a round, baby face.

'Sit, gentlemen,' Cheep waved a hand magnanimously as

chairs were shuffled and the seats of uniform trousers were lifted an inch or two. 'Thank you Harry,' Cheep accepted the chair at the head of the gleaming table which Curtiss obediently held for him. They made an odd pair, Cheep the bantam cock in his full uniform, crown and pip sparkling on his epaulettes; Curtiss, overweight, a hulk in a sagging tunic.

'Now then,' Cheep rubbed his hands, 'to business . . . no time for idle chit-chat, we've got the finest bloody division in this police force to run here and I aim to keep it that way.' He shuffled his papers, 'we've got a big agenda to get through, so let's get the spark plugs firing, 'kay!'

It was the same homily he delivered every time and Curtiss noticed the usual dismayed glances around the table.

One by one the sub-divisional chief inspectors delivered concise little speeches on their various responsibilities and Cheep brushed each one aside with a curt, 'fine . . . fine . . . just keep on the ball, OK?'

When that part of the proceedings had been completed, Cheep told them: 'Now you men think you're pretty damn sharp, eh? Keep the old man happy with a lot of soft soap, tell him what he wants to hear. Well I've got news for you. I hear rumblings . . .' he pointed towards the window '. . . out there. Members of the public who've seen policemen sloppily dressed. Officers without caps. No seat belts in the pandas, and that kind of thing. That's loose management and it's got to stop – understand? Otherwise one of these fine days some panda bandit's going to draw an official complaint and we don't have complaints on S Division. That's rule number one. Now when you get back to your stations you get onto it, crack down on your sergeants, put the fear of Christ into 'em. If we have a complaint go through to headquarters, we get a black mark like that, and someone's head's going to roll. So don't come here trying to pull the wool over my eyes, 'kay!' He turned to Curtiss. 'Harry, what's this comedy the dog handlers are trying here. You seriously expect me to send this up to Policy?' He brandished a neatly typed report from the dog section requesting the official issue of light coloured jeans for officers engaged in police dog training duties.

I HEAR RUMBLINGS

'We'd be a laughing stock.' Cheep glowered around the table. 'Which comedian put this up?'

At the far end one of the inspectors cleared his throat. 'Sir – I had an approach from one of the dog sergeants – he says because they're training their dogs in uniform, they'll only go for suspects in dark trousers. So I just thought . . .'

'Now you listen,' Cheep cut him off thumping the table with his fist. 'Nobody's making a monkey out've me. You take that back to your dog sergeant and tell him where he can stick it – 'kay!' He sent the report skimming down the table and the Inspector sheepishly retrived it as Cheep raised a hand to his forehead and inserted a little finger under his artificial hairline and scratched vigorously. 'When I need dog handlers to get smart with me I'll give 'em Bonio to chew on . . . tell 'em that from me.'

He looked down at his papers. 'OK – what's next?' His eyes seized on an item he had underlined in red and he rounded on Brian Webber, the Detective Chief Inspector who ran the S Division CID. 'Oh yes . . . what's all this Webber!' Cheep slapped a sheaf of crime reports and his voice rose an octave. 'How many times do I have to tell you – S division has the best clear-up rate in the force, bar none. Now what d'you think you're doing? You're giving me a whole heap of nothing here Webber. Look at this . . . look at this!' Cheep flipped through the pages with a growing air of disgust. 'Petty theft, Peanut burglaries, flashers. . . . Christ alight, you crime this lot and our figures'll go off the scale. I won't tell you again, you only crime the stuff we can detect, that way the detection rate stays good and healthy and everybody's happy. The rest of this junk,' Cheep produced a low moan, 'You've got to get rid of it. . . understand? What's the matter with those zombies out there you call detectives. Jesus, since when couldn't a detective worth his salt talk a complainant out've making it official when he could see as plain as the nose on his face that he don't have a cat in hell's chance of clearing the job. Mother of Christ, do I have to spell it out to you dumb-bells every time? You want to stick a torpedo into my crime statistics or something? You want to go back to those days when we had those nit-pickers from headquarters beating about the undergrowth and making all our lives a misery?' Cheep assumed an expression as though he was talking to a backward child. 'Look Brian,' he began familiarly, 'just do it my way, 'kay? Bury this stuff somewhere it won't show and don't ever go sending up a crime-state like this again. In S Division we clear *all* our crime. That makes you and your boys the best detectives in the force. Be proud of that Brian, and don't go looking for ulcers or you'll have me to contend with – do I make myself clear?'

Webber stood his ground under Cheep's withering attack. He was a young man with fair hair and an easy pleasant manner, but his jaw tightened as he said: 'Sir – we've got a missing girl, a 14-year-old over on the Eastgate estate, adrift five days now. Should I tell her parents to forget it?'

'Don't get sharp with me Webber,' Cheep snapped. 'You might cut yourself. I read the file on that one and I don't see any problem. You've put out a MISPER. She's circulated.'

'What I think Chief Inspector Webber is saying,' Curtiss spoke for the first time, 'is that from the inquiries we've made so far, there's growing concern for this kid's safety. We've got a witness who says there was a car kerb crawling in the area and she never went missing before. Just went out to visit a friend and never came back.'

'I know that Harry,' said Cheep peevishly. 'But we've done everything according to the book. We've circulated her.'

'I think Brian here feels we should step up the response – get a major enquiry going.'

'Oh no you don't,' Cheep's eyes narrowed. 'With the duty scheme the way it is, that'd mean overtime and I'm not burning up the allocation playing hide and seek with some jailbait.'

Anxious glances were exchanged around the table as Cheep exhaled an exasperated sigh. 'All I can say is you've got damned short memories. Look what happened out on V last year when that bird went on the trot and everybody got 'emselves steamed up, press, tv, mass searches, the military, the whole circus. Then they found her shacked up with some jungle bunny in the Met having a whale of a time. Remember?' Cheep wagged his head sagely. 'The county got stung with a whopping great bill and the chief came out've the Police Committee with his arse in his hand. You want an action replay of that fiasco!'

'As I recall,' Harry Curtiss observed drily, 'the female in that incident was a 19-year-old scrubber.'

'Sir,' Webber chipped in, unable to contain himself further, 'we're talking about a girl of 14 who never even went to the Girl Guides without her father took her. She wouldn't say boo to a goose.'

'Hey!' Cheep exploded. 'Don't you go 14-year-olding me son. I've seen 'em 14, tits out here.' She's probably shacked up somewhere and when she gets tired of it she'll come home and that's all there is to it. When that happens we might get a USI out've it, but until then we're going to leave it at a MISPER – understand!'

There was a moment's silence and then Cheep said: 'Well now we've got all that garbage in the can I've got some good news for you. I was talking to the chief the other day . . . oh, he was asking my advice on this and that . . .' Cheep puffed out his chest in pride, 'and I told him what we need right now is a big public relations campaign, something with a bit of zing in it and the old man said to me "Maxwell," he said, "you're just the man to take that under your wing". So I told him he could count on S Division a hundred per cent.' Cheep leaned back and examined their blank expressions. 'You know what I said? I told him we could have the public eating out've our hands if we can pull off PAPA.' Cheep was by now gazing at the ceiling and so missed their incredulous expressions.

'PAPA?' Curtiss tried the word tentatively.

'PAPA!' Cheep lowered his eyes triumphantly. 'Police and Public Action – got to have a good catchy slogan for a campaign. I just took that one off the top of my head . . . it's got a good paternal ring to it.'

Curtiss, who wondered at first if this wasn't a lead up to some elaborate joke, could see from his chief's expression that he was quite serious.

'PAPA.' Curtiss pronounced the word again and made it sound like a groan.

'See Harry, you're getting the feel of it already,' said Cheep, so elated by his own display of genius that he completely missed the tone of his deputy's voice. 'My friends,' he continued expansively, 'we've got a chance here to really set this police force alight. The chief's given me a free hand for a pilot campaign on this division, so by God we're really going to make PAPA work.' He rubbed his hands enthusiastically and ran an expectant glance around the table. 'OK – who's got some bright ideas?'

He fixed his gaze on one of the sub-divisional Chief Inspectors who wriggled uncomfortably and suggested a public open day at his station, show the folks the cells and the handcuffs, that sort of thing. Someone else said he might organise a display of police badges of which he was a noted collector. Then there was an embarrassed silence.

'All right,' Cheep said finally, 'I suppose I'm going to have to do everything myself – well, I'm pretty used to that.' He opened a bright orange folder, reviewed its contents and then said: 'So this is *my* plan. We're going to make this the friendly division where the police and the public are one big happy family. You'd better make notes of this. One – every officer will be instructed to smile whenever he's dealing with the public. Two – we're going to draw up a happy-hour scheme; meetings, coffee mornings, and things like that. Three – we're going to have posters and stickers – particularly stickers – with catchy designs and not just in the stations but everywhere, even on the pandas. Four – someone can organise the community associations to write in letters of support for the file. Five – for the kids we'll have street parties, sponsored table tennis and good wholesome games. Well, there's a few ideas for you to get started with. Now I want all your plans submitted to my office within the next couple of days.' He consulted his diary. 'Because we're going to strike while the iron's hot. We'll run the PAPA campaign all next month so you've got 10 days to set it up. And I want to be really impressed with your initiative. . . .' A cunning look crossed

Cheep's face. 'You might like to bear in mind that it's coming around to annual reports again and I wouldn't like to think of any of you not pulling your weight – 'kay!'

They were too stunned to speak as Cheep added: 'And remember those smiles, the PAPA smiles. A good policeman is a smiling policeman – right! Oh and you needn't concern yourself with the publicity. I'll take care of that personally – it's right up my street. Press conferences, radio, tv, the whole works, that'll really make headquarters sit up.'

He flopped back in his chair as though exhausted from his own brilliance in outlining his master plan. 'All right,' he said finally, 'that's it – count-down to PAPA. I don't think I need detain you any longer gentlemen, unless anyone has a particular point to raise.' He looked around the table again. No one spoke. Eyes were averted as his gaze traversed the group.

Finally Cheep told them: 'A good meeting I think gentlemen. Let's keep right on our toes – 'kay!' He pushed his chair back and stood up looking down on Curtiss: 'Oh bring my papers through would you Harry,' turned on his heel and left the conference room.

When Maxwell Cheep was safely out of earshot a low groan reverberated around the table. 'Jesus,' one of them murmured, expressing the shared opinion, 'we're going to get crucified on this. How're we going to get hairy arsed bobbies to *smile* for God's sake.'

'PAPA,' someone breathed the slogan experimentally. 'Oh Jesus Christ . . . tell me I dreamed it.'

As the meeting broke up Webber took Curtiss to one side and said: 'Harry I'm going to have to ask to see the old man again. Make him understand this missing girl is a serious business. If it goes sour we could get taken to the cleaners – I've got to make him see that.'

Curtiss chewed his lip and then replied: 'Leave it for a bit Brian. I'll have a go at him, see if I can't make him see sense. I know you've got a bad feeling about this and . . .'

'I'm telling you Harry,' Webber exclaimed angrily. 'Something's got to be done about him. Talk about a divisional commander, he couldn't even run a piss-up in a brewery.'

Curtiss frowned. He had been steeped in the traditions of the service and didn't just see Cheep the man, he saw the insignia on the uniform. Rank counted and try as he might, he couldn't change the unswerving loyalties of a lifetime. 'Brian – in the circumstances I'm going to forget you said that,' he replied not unkindly, 'you're upset and I understand that, but don't let me hear you criticising a senior officer again, otherwise I'm not going to be able to ignore it.' He was in an invidious position as Cheep's deputy and the dilemma gnawed at him constantly. 'Look,' he told the detective in a conciliatory manner, 'I'll do my best for you Brian and I'll get back to you as soon as I can. I'll work something out.'

When they had all gone, Curtiss gathered up Cheep's papers and determined to tackle the divisional commander right away, perhaps barter a little more effort on the missing girl inquiry for enthusiasm for the PAPA campaign. He knew from past experience that the best way to reach Cheep was with a trade-off and he hoped he possessed sufficient guile to make it stick. He went through into the commander's outer office where Mrs Moravia, Cheep's harridan of a secretary barred the way to the inner sanctum. Mrs Moravia (her Christian name had been long forgotten) was a shrivelled-up shrew who jealously guarded her domain. No one knew how long she had held her job. No one had been around long enough to remember.

'Chief in his office?' Curtiss asked of her as a preliminary to the inquisition which preceeded any request for an audience with little God. Without looking up from her IBM, Mrs Moravia jerked a thumb towards the commander's private bathroom, and Curtiss knowing it would be pointless to proceed further, dropped Cheep's papers on her desk and returned to his own office down the corridor, his brow creased with private thoughts of which one in particular was dominant: it certainly wasn't the job he'd joined all those years ago.

* * *

Behind the locked door of that most private of all private

places, Maxwell Cheep was very pleased with himself that morning as he sat on the toilet and stared at his knees. His doctor had told him he had what was known as a relaxed colon which necessitated several visits to the loo each day, but which did not disturb him unduly for he found that such necessity had greatly enhanced his power of meditation. Well, he'd certainly shown those wiseacres a thing or two. You didn't get to the high reaches of command by sitting around shuffling paper, you had to have drive, imagination, a will to succeed. PAPA was a master stroke, Cheep was convinced of that, it was just what the force needed right now, a bright PR image. Put those bastards who kept sniping in the newspapers about imagined shortcomings, right in their place. A subtle manoeuvre to win the hearts and minds of the public.

Oh yes indeed. And S Division leading the way. The chief would be proud of him and it would certainly strengthen his lobby for an OBE, or at the very least, the Queen's Police Medal. Cheep hadn't told those numbskulls yet, but privately he planned a big reception to launch the PAPA campaign, inviting MPs, civic dignitaries, members of the Police Authority Committee. A tasteful affair, he thought, something they would remember him for. Might even have lapel pins made . . . he'd think about that one. Yes, he'd really make a name for himself with PAPA. The publicity potential was enormous, of that he was convinced. He'd read books on the subject. Oh yes indeed, it was going to be his year all right. Why, he was already president of the county golf club and his wife was lady president, a double achievement which had gone down as a record in the annals of the club's revered history.

Cheep felt contented, but as his contentment grew, his mind wandered back to the thoughts which had dominated his waking hours for a month or more. Christine Lowe, the girl from the typing pool. His mouth began to dry up and his breathing became laboured as he thought of her, his erotic fantasy returning in vivid technicolour. Christine Lowe, naked and exciting, spreadeagled on top of his wide mahogany executive desk with him tucking it to her with all the virility of a young stud. Cheep sighed heavily at the images his mind created, raised a hand and removed his wig so that he could massage his balding pate. Ah . . . Christine Lowe, with her long blonde hair, angelic schoolgirl face, firm young breasts and leggy provacative walk. A mournful sigh escaped his lips.

Like many such flights of middle-aged passion, it had begun innocently enough when Mrs Moravia (who had never succumbed to sickness in her life) asked for a day off to attend an aunt's funeral. It was not a question of sentimentally, she told Cheep bluntly, just the necessity of a physical presence when the spoils of the old lady's home were divided up. If she wasn't there she would undoubtedly forfeit her share with those vultures around, explained Mrs Moravia, who had never before asked for time off apart from her annual holiday when a stand-in of suitable competence was always drafted in from headquarters. She further informed Cheep that she was not requesting the time off, she was entitled to it as a right under her terms of employment.

In ill humour at this unexpected hiccup in the smooth running of his office, Cheep had demanded a typist from the pool to cover the day in question. The girl assigned by S Division administration turned out to be Christine Lowe.

Now Christine's personal file was more concerned with her secretarial qualifications; good accurate typing, fair shorthand speed, than her less tangible attributes which were considerable. She wore her bleached hair long, down to the shoulder, her face, while not exactly pretty had other more basic attractions, a wide sensuous mouth, large almond eyes accentuated by the skilful use of shadow and mascara; a well-endowed girl whose breasts verged on the pendulous, shaping down to narrow hips and long curvy legs which were without doubt her very best feature. Nor was Christine unaware of her ability to turn men's heads. At the tender age of 22 she had been twice married, divorced once and now legally separated, was too smart to have conceived within her smooth flat belly and possessed more than the average share of feminine wiles. During her 12 months as an S Division administration typist, she had dallied with most of the eligible men on the station and quite a few who weren't, in return for a good night out or other

I WOULD LIKE YOU TO TAKE SOMETHING DOWN MISS LOWE

favours, to enhance the pleasant flavour of her carefree existence.

When Maxwell Cheep had pressed the summons key on his dictograph on the morning of Mrs Moravia's absence and Christine Lowe swivelled into his office with her notebook and pencil, he fell in love with her at first sight.

During the course of that fateful day Cheep contrived to dictate numerous letters, memos and reports. He couldn't take his eyes off her and Christine for her part soon became aware of her effect on little God. She began to tease him, tossing her hair so that it swished, placing the end of her pencil between her lips suggestively when their eyes met as Cheep paused between sentences. Deliberately crossing and uncrossing her legs to the rustle of nylon. Cheep began to move around the office as he dictated, breathing shallowly as lust engulfed him. He grew bolder, complimented her on her appearance, even laid a hand on her shoulder in a fatherly gesture, smiled and laughed a lot. She found the interlude pleasantly amusing, and when late in the afternoon Cheep finally plucked up his courage and patted her knee, she rose swiftly from her chair and succeeded in brushing a hand across his groin as she passed him on her way out of the office for the last time. His response was instant, and Maxwell Cheep sat slumped in his ox-blood hide executive chair for a full half hour after she had gone home, panting lightly and unable to concentrate on the mountain of paperwork he had generated in the course of the day. She had bewitched him.

That evening he scowled at his wife and uncharacteristically brushed aside her anecdotes of golfing prowess which had formerly always filled him with pride. He surveyed his boney, unlovely, middle-aged mate with a jaundiced eye and ached for Christine Lowe. But Mrs Moravia was back in her chair the following morning, all brisk and businesslike, and as he watched her despatch the fruits of his previous day's labour with her usual brusque efficiency, Maxwell Cheep felt his heart sink. He knew from experience that he would never unseat Mrs Moravia and so raise his beloved Christine to his side. The best he could hope for was a tantalising glimpse of her on one of his forays around the station. He had his position to think of and he agonised inwardly for it seemed that fate had delivered him a particularly cruel blow.

But there was something else of which Maxell Cheep was blissfully unaware as he sat in his private bathroom contemplating his knees, dreaming his lurid dreams. Christine Lowe was none too discreet. She had talked to one of her friends in the typing pool about her interlude in the divisional commander's office and although no actual rumour had developed, the news of Cheep's predilection for the long-legged Christine reached certain ears and like all useful police intelligence, was carefully stored away for future evaluation. Cheep sighed as he completed his toilet, diligently washing his hands and face then inspecting his countenance in the wash basin mirror. Fervently he prayed for some stroke of luck, some act of God which would rid him of that harridan in his outer office so that he could engineer Christine Lowe's promotion. In the meantime he would throw himself into his work, flesh out a few of his brilliant ideas for the PAPA campaign.

He went through into his office, made himself comfortable behind his desk and opened the orange folder. He reached across to the dictograph and buzzed Mrs Moravia. 'No calls or visitors,' he snapped. 'I'm concentrating on important work, 'kay!' Mrs Moravia merely grunted. She didn't even bother to tell Cheep that Harry Curtiss had been looking for him.

* * *

There was much wailing and gnashing of teeth when the senior officers of S Division attempted to inform the troops of the PAPA campaign. Somehow Maxwell Cheep's grand design to enhance the image of his men in the eyes of the public would not translate into the earthy monosyllabic speech pattern which served as the basic form of communication down the chain of command. For a while the S Division hierarchy fell back in disarray. Then, when all else had failed the sub-divisional chief inspectors called in their inspectors and informed them that bright careers in the force could be jeopardised if little God's plans were not smoothly implemented. The inspectors went back to their respective stations, called in their section sergeants and spelled out to them in no uncertain terms that if they had any aspirations towards wearing two pips on their shoulders, they'd better damn well get their fingers out on this one because the old man was screaming for blood. Suitably impressed by this textbook gem of man-management, the supervisory sergeants paraded their shifts of constables, screamed and bellowed and tore their hair whilst imparting the message that if they didn't knuckle under and put some beef into the chief superintendent's crackpot idea, they'd get their arses kicked from here to breakfast time. Thus informed, the constables returned to their duties and an air of sullen resentment settled over the division.

When Harry Curtiss finally managed to slip under Mrs Moravia's guard and raise the question of the missing girl with the divisional commander, Maxwell Cheep looked up from admiring the artwork for his PAPA posters and car stickers which were set out on his desk and responded irritably: 'Harry – I thought I'd made myself crystal clear on that one.'

'Webber's very concerned sir,' Curtiss replied, 'He's very conscientious and I really think we ought . . .'

'What!' Cheep cut him short. 'Those CID cowboys must think I was born yesterday. Oh I see right through their little game – they're just looking for a licence to print money. Well, they're not milking the overtime allotment while I'm in the chair. Not for some toe-rag with hot knickers they're not.'

Abruptly dismissing the subject Cheep wave a hand across the glossy layout. 'What d'you think of these beauties, eh Harry? A minor masterpiece in promotional artwork.'

Curtiss took in the pictures and slogans for the first time. He couldn't believe his eyes. Everywhere there was the face of a fresh handsome young man in police uniform, smiling an innocent beatific smile which displayed perfectly even white teeth. He looked so unlike any policeman Curtiss had ever seen that before he could stop himself, the superintendent blurted out: 'Where did you get him from sir? I never knew we had coppers who looked like that!'

'Don't be a prat all your life Harry,' replied Cheep scathingly, 'you don't use any old copper for a thing like this . . . you use a model.'

'A male model!' Curtiss was astounded.

'Best in the business,' said Cheep, admiring the pictures, 'got the kind of face people put their trust in . . . just perfect for the campaign don't you think Harry?'

His mind reeling from this latest piece of sacrilege, a male model in police uniform, Curtiss could only manage a strangled: 'Sir I don't think the lads . . . .'

'The lads,' Cheep laughed derisively, 'you didn't seriously expect to see one of their ugly mugs here did you? Maybe a broken nose or a cauliflower ear? Come on . . . grow up will you,' Cheep mocked his deputy. 'We're talking about a clean cut image, not some horror film production.' He waved Curtiss away: 'Go on Harry, you just keep the wheels oiled, keep the old clockwork ticking away, and don't start offering opinions on things you don't understand . . . leave the brainwork to me 'kay!'

When Curtiss had gone Cheep picked up the artwork and began fitting the slogans to the pictures. Below the improbably perfect face ran the legend: 'Smile for PAPA – POLICE AND PUBLIC ACTION – Make friends with the police – we're on your side'. He puffed out his chest with pride. The sentiment he had spent so much time polishing seemed just about right.

* * *

There were posters everywhere; smiling out from the windows of shops and libraries, adorning notice boards outside police stations and public buildings, exhorting the public from hoardings and even the door panels of Pandas and other police vehicles. Grinning devilishly, the S. Division PCs handed out car stickers to everything that moved. By the day after the big reception and press conference, Maxwell Cheep was walking 10 feet tall. Already PAPA was exceeding his wildest dreams. He had appeared on television twice, had listened to his own recorded interview on the radio and had seen his picture in most of the papers. He had even heard that little old ladies were writing in to the chief constable congratulating the force on its cheerful disposition. Maxwell Cheep felt a rosy glow of well-being settle over him.

But with all the subtlety of a chameleon adjusting to changes in its environment, the canteen mafia was preparing for guerilla warfare and by day three of the PAPA campaign, contingency plans were completed and they were ready for action. Overnight a counter campaign was launched. Crudely lettered posters hideously caricaturing the PAPA publicity bearing the slogan CRAP – Campaign for the Return to Active Policing – began to appear as quickly as they could be illicitly produced on station photocopiers.

At first a rash of CRAP posters mysteriously materialised inside the police stations, on bulletin boards and the walls of corridors. Newspapers and the television station received them anonymously through the post. Here and there in public places PAPA posters had their CRAP counterparts pasted over them. The S Division brass, fearing terrible retribution, endeavoured to conceal this appalling turn of events from little God. They raced around like dervishes tearing down the offending posters, but like the Hydra, whenever one was destroyed two more sprang up in its place. In desperation they pleaded with the troops to abandon this childish gesture of contempt which could only bring trouble for them all, but the seasoned campaigners among the lower ranks replied with innocently-raised eyebrows and complete indifference. Finally the chief inspectors on the sub-divisions called Harry Curtiss.

'What!' Curtiss came out of his chair like a rocket, clutching the 'phone so tightly his knuckles whitened. 'you're joking! What! Jesus, the newspapers too? – and the TV! Oh my God, the old man'll blow a bloody gasket. Listen . . . listen . . . . you get the men together and you tell 'em from me that Federation or no Federation, unless they stop this little game right now, I'm going to personally make it my business to come down there and kick seven bells out've every bastard I connect with this. I'll bust every one of 'em to traffic warden and that's if they're lucky. You tell 'em that from me!' Suddenly Curtiss felt his loyalty flagging and he sat down heavily, still clutching the 'phone as the anger went out of his voice. 'See what you can do anyway, but to tell you the truth I've got a lot of sympathy with the lads, only I can't show it otherwise discipline's going right out of the window.'

Curtiss sat for a long moment staring at the telephone and winding up his courage to face the divisional commander. He need not have worried because when he eventually approached the inner sanctum, Mrs Moravia told him without looking up from her IBM: 'He's not in to anybody – put it in a memo'.

But it was only a matter of time before Maxwell Cheep learned of the CRAP sabotage when he took a call from one of his newspaper cronies who asked whether he had any comment to make on what appeared to be an elaborate practical joke. Choleric with fury, Cheep spent time in his bathroom and then summoned Curtiss to the presence.

'Harry,' he said, his face white with rage. 'If these jokers think they're going to pull a stroke like this and get away with it, they're very much mistaken. Either every one of those . . . those *things* go or I'm going to start handing down discipline charges like confetti. They're going to wish they'd never been born, is that clear?' Cheep wagged a finger in a threatening gesture. 'And I'll tell you something else Harry, if this nonsense isn't over and forgotten by next Monday morning, I'll put every other man on the sheet for "conduct unbecoming" and fine 'em a month's pay. That should set 'em at each other's throats. Divide and conquer Harry . . . divide and conquer.'

Before Curtiss could reply Cheep was out of his chair and heading for the bathroom. It was too much for a relaxed colon to withstand. Alone in the divisional commander's office, Curtiss found himself once more reflecting upon the past glories which the surroundings evoked. He remembered the old chief in this very room, ruling the Borough Force with a rod of iron and as he looked around reminiscing to himself, a plan so diabolicial that it caused him to tremble, began to form in his mind. And at last Harry Curtiss knew he could bend the code he had lived by for so long if by so doing he would preserve the traditions he held so dear. Otherwise the division would be torn to pieces by internal strife, the laughing stock of the rest of the force. As the plan began to take root, Curtiss convinced himself that he had to give it a try or else go down with the sinking ship.

* * *

On Thursday of that week as the PAPA v CRAP controversy flared and ebbed, Mrs Moravia (who had never had a day's illness in her life) complained that the coffee had a peculiar taste. The following morning she 'phoned in sick having spent a wretched night vomiting without relief. The doctor said she must have picked up a bug or else it was something she had eaten. Maxwell Cheep was most sympathetic, but secretly he couldn't believe his good fortune. The moment she was off the telephone he reached for the dictograph with a hand which trembled slightly and asked Admin to send up a temporary secretary.

'The girl who came up before,' he said as offhandedly as he could manage, 'what was her name now, ah yes . . . Miss Lowe. She knows how my office runs, send her up immediately would you.'

Cheep was so overjoyed that he temporarily forgot his feud with the lower ranks. A whole day with *her!* He began to shake so badly at the mere thought of it that it required a conscious effort to pull himself together.

Christine Lowe took the news of her temporary assignment with similar enthusiasm. She had been informed in a roundabout way that if she played her cards right with Cheepie (as the divisional commander was familiarly known to the typing pool) she could expect to advance at least two increments on her Local Government pay scale. Before she went up to start work, she slipped into the powder room and touched up her eye make-up and lipstick with particular care. A rise of two increments was not to be sneezed at.

'Why Miss Lowe,' Cheep was effusive when she presented herself in his outer office. 'This is nice, don't you think?' His voice took on a simpering tone as Christine fluttered her eyelashes. 'Perhaps we'll get to known each other better eh? You don't mind if I call you Christine?'

They flirted with each other throughout the day, Cheep laughing a lot and venturing whenever possible to squeeze her hand with an intimate gesture. Christine Lowe moistened her pearly pink lips with the tip of her tongue, smoothed her blue wet-look blouse to accentuate the slope of her breasts, allowed her skirt to ride up over her knees to reveal the curve of her long legs. Languidly dictating his correspondence Cheep found himself experiencing hot and cold flushes.

Towards the end of the afternoon when she had laughed at his joke about the Jewish Kamikazi pilot who crashed his plane into his brother's scrapyard, Cheep summoned up the nerve to broach the proposition which had been on his mind all day.

'I was wondering Christine,' he began, trying to keep his voice from betraying his excitement, 'whether you were in a hurry to get away this evening. Boyfriend . . . something like that?'

Christine Lowe explored the end of her pencil with the tip of her tongue before replying that her time was her own and that she had no pressing reason to leave on time.

'Because,' Cheep cleared his throat, 'I thought we could perhaps work over for an hour or so – have a little drinkie, perhaps?'

She regarded him from under her eyelashes and told him she was happy to help out in any way she could.

And so at some time after six when the divisional commander could be confident that the top corridor was deserted, he crossed the office to his hospitality cabinet and proposed a drink, just to unwind. Christine Lowe asked for a Bacardi and Coke, but settled for a gin and tonic. When he refilled her glass for a second time, Maxwell Cheep could stand the suspense no longer. He seized her by the shoulders and kissed her clumsily, clashing teeth in his haste, but instead of pulling back as he had feared, Christine drew him to her, her hands moving down his back as she returned his kiss expertly, her tongue darting into his mouth.

Cheep felt he might swoon as he tried feverishly to embrace her, but she murmured in his ear . . . 'What if someone should come?'

Panting lightly, he scurried from the office and after surreptitiously checking that that floor was indeed deserted, discreetly locked the outer door as he returned, his heart hammering furiously.

Christine Lowe turned to meet him and the sight caused him to break out in a light sweat as he tried in vain to swallow the lump in his throat which threatened to choke him. Her blouse was open to the waist, somehow her bra had disappeared, and as he moved towards her, floating it seemed, unaware of his legs beneath him, she gave a small shrug of her shoulders and the blouse swung open unveiling those smooth perfect breasts.

Cheep felt dizzy, his head reeling, his knees weak as she embraced him and whispered: 'A girl ought to be proud of her body . . . don't you think?'

But he couldn't reply for she had guided his head against her breast and his mouth was around a nipple the size of a walnut. Time lost all meaning for Maxwell Cheep. In the blink of an eye, or so it seemed, Christine had wriggled out of her skirt and slipped off her tights, leaving him to fumble with lacy panties as she nimbly undressed him.

'Over here,' she murmured huskily, leading him towards an open space of carpet, 'and don't worry about a thing . . . I'm on the pill.'

'No. . . NO,' Cheep managed to croak as his erotic fantasy returned, firing his imagination, 'please. . . please . . . on the desk!'

Cheep swept the clutter aside with abandon and for a second saw her there before him, spreadeagled on the dark mahogany, his lustful gaze roving over creamy thighs before he was on top of her, his toupee wildly askew, face buried between those firm inviting breasts as Christine Lowe, whispering soothing encouragement, entwined her long legs around his waist, drawing him in to her, arching her back to set them into motion which began slowly and then rose smoothly to the frantic see-sawing of a rider astride a bucking broncho.

Maxwell Cheep felt himself soaring towards ecstasy. He had no way of knowing that the trapdoor of the dumb waiter adjacent to the desk had slid open a fraction, that in the shaft which was just wide enough to accommodate a man, a surveillance camera fitted with a wide-angle lens was being trained through the narrow opening. Nor as he moaned his expression of raw passion did he hear the soft whirr of the motorised Pentax. He was too far gone.

* * *

After a pleasant week-end bathing in the glory of his new-found virility, Maxwell Cheep drove to the S Division headquarters earlier than usual on Monday morning, full of vigour and determined to put down the CRAP rebellion by implementing his draconian measures. He parked in his reserved place in the car park and strutted into the mansion, taking pleasure from the bustle and confusion his unheralded arrival had created. He even bade Mrs Moravia a cheerful good morning and inquired after her health as he went through into his office.

Cheep sat at his desk and was about to buzz Harry Curtiss and order the commencement of disciplinary proceedings when he noticed a brown manilla envelope propped against his ornate brass ink-stand. Odd, he thought. Mrs Moravia always dealt with the post. He turned the envelope over in his hands. It was addressed to him in large anonymous capitals. Interesting, Cheep thought, his curiosity aroused. He took his paper knife and slit the envelope and the contents spilled out into the desk. Glossy photographs, printed eight by ten. He took one look and his blood turned to ice, his head began to ring, his breath became laboured and his genitals shrivelled as he gasped in horror.

The pictures were all different but the subject was the same. There, captured in two-dimensional monochrome on top of that very desk was himself, naked but for his socks, white shanks and buttocks in the foreground and his own unmistakable face, wig tilted ludicrously over one eye framed between ample breasts as he 'tucked it' to Christine Lowe. With a strangled sob Maxwell Cheep looked frantically around the room and then his eyes settled on the sliding door of the dumb waiter. He began to moan in anguish as he desperately shuffled the photographs looking for some sort of origin, some clue, blackmail demand . . . anything! There was not even a note.

* * *

At about the same time in a far flung corner of the S Division, a 19-year-old probationary constable who needed to shave only once every three days was diligently distributing PAPA car stickers much to the chagrin of his colleagues who regarded him as a traitor to the cause having ditched their stickers down the nearest drain. He had blue eyes and ruddy cheeks and might have followed their example if he hadn't been terrified of the section sergeant who, acting on instructions from above, had successfully put the 'fear of Christ' into him. As it was, he disposed of his stickers as quickly as he could, pressing them on to motorists whether they agreed or not, whilst smiling a vacuous smile in the best PAPA image.

To speed the task even further he also slapped the stickers on every unattended vehicle he could find and when he walked into an alleyway between some shops and found an old Ford saloon parked against some hoardings, he reached into his fast diminishing supply and went to work. The driver's door was unlocked and so he stuck a sticker on the windscreen and another on the dashboard for good measure. He walked around the car, practising his measured gait and on impulse tried the boot. The lock clicked open and the lid rose on its spring revealing a sight which sent the young policeman reeling back, his eyes wide, his breakfast coming up into his mouth. Curled up in the boot, the scant remains of her clothing torn and blood-spattered, was the corpse of the fourteen year old girl missing from the Eastgate Estate. She had been criminally assaulted and stabbed to death with a screwdriver.

Three The Inspection

'RUM sort of cove that Cheep fellow,' the HMI reflected over a pink gin in the mess. 'Looked like he'd been on night manoeuvres for a week.'

'Yes,' replied Henry Grey, stroking his bristling moustache with a forefinger. He too had been astonished by Maxwell Cheep's catatonic demeanour. 'We had high hopes of him. Seems to have gone completely to pieces.'

Sir Ralph Hawk's bushy eyebrows knitted into a serious expression: 'Responsibility of command Henry. Takes a special kind of backbone. Weeds the men out from the boys.'

'I can't imagine what's got into him Sir Ralph,' Grey said. 'He's always been . . . well . . . so enthusiastic.'

'Weighs heavy,' said Sir Ralph, staring into his glass.

'Sir?'

'Responsibility of command,' repeated the HMI.

'Oh I quite agree,' Grey said.

'Need to select your men with a clear eye and sound judgement,' said Sir Ralph. 'No room for sentiment.'

'No Sir Ralph,' Grey said, as he tried to decide whether or not the HMI's comment carried an implied rebuke. 'None at all.'

The inspection had been going so well, Grey thought to himself, everything in apple pie order, report books laid out just so, officers spruced up and alert, Superintendent Curtiss dancing attendance at a respectful distance. Then that idiot Cheep had to go and let the side down, pale as death warmed up, standing around like a zombie and obliging Sir Ralph to repeat his questions, and rushing off to the bathroom like that every few minutes. His conduct was unforgivable, quite unforgivable.

Of course the deputy chief constable was blissfully unaware of the realities of the situation at the S Division headquarters; the cajoling and browbeating with which Curtiss had prepared the route of the inspection tour. As always it was a cosmetic operation and if the HMI had deviated from the official path then he would have stumbled upon a scene of disorder and chaos. It was rather like walking over an ant-hill, impervious to the frenzied activity going on underfoot.

'I'd take a close look at Cheep,' Sir Ralph said draining his glass. 'It's up to us Henry to maintain the high standards of the service.'

Grey nodded vigorously as he signalled a white gloved cadet hovering nearby to replenish the HMI's drink.

'Oh I'll get onto it right away Sir Ralph.'

'Give those personnel fellows a roasting.'

'Absolutely. I'll take care of it Sir Ralph.'

'Clear eye and sound judgement. They were always my watchword when selecting commanders.'

'You're so right Sir Ralph.'

The HMI frowned as a fragment of memory came back to him, his eyes almost disappearing under a thicket of eyebrows.

'Was I mistaken Henry,' he began slowly as though some appalling truth had just dawned upon him, 'or was that Cheep person actually wearing a wig. . .?'

Four The Arrow Bridge Jumper

THE PC who found the body in the boot of the car was called Nigel Butt. Right afterwards he reported sick with nervous exhaustion and was off the duty scheme for the best part of six weeks. The doctors called it some fancy name like trauma shock, but really it was nothing of the sort. When Nigel Butt looked down into the boot recess of that beat-up Mark I Cortina and saw a pale dead face staring back at him, he was immediately reminded of the Arrow Bridge jumper and that was more than he could bear.

Like so many kids of his generation, weaned on the Welfare State, Nigel Butt was a strapping six footer with fair hair, an engaging smile and a well compensated personality. He had a good head on his shoulders too and did so well in the academic sixth of one of the county's better grammar schools, that the careers counsellor began mapping out a bright future in commerce or industry. But there was one snag. Ever since he could remember, Nigel Butt had had one burning ambition and try as they might, no-one, family, friends or tutors, could steer him off his chosen course. He was determined to become a policeman.

'What d'you want to do?' his father finally exploded in exasperation, 'get your head kicked in down an alley one night. . .?'

'Dad . . . I want to help. I want to help people. . . .'

'So be a bank manager and help people,' said his father who had only made chief cashier and cherished the hope that he could vicariously reach the boss's chair through his son. 'Money . . . that's the best way to help people.'

'You don't understand. . . .'

'Oh yes I do. Kids these days . . . you think you know it all. What's being a policeman going to do for you eh? Except break your mother's heart.'

'I just want to help people Dad.'

'So what's wrong with the bank . . . tell me that?'

'Nothing's wrong with the bank.'

'We sacrificed ourselves for you . . . your mother and me,'

said his father, resorting to the oldest form of parental blackmail. 'Now you turn around and give us a slap in the face like this.'

'I just want to do something useful with my life Dad.'

'Oh Christ!'

'I want to find out what makes people tick.'

'Oh yeah! By locking 'em up!'

'Dad it isn't like that any more.'

'Like hell it isn't!'

And so at 17, having finally talked his parents around, Nigel Butt joined the force as a cadet and spent the happiest year of his life; sailing, canoeing, studying, and generally cutting a fine figure in his spruce blue uniform. During his practical attachments he rode in pandas and traffic cars, put on a sports jacket and walked the streets with the detectives, soaked up the salty gossip in the canteen. He loved every minute of it and nobody was in the least surprised when on the day of the passing out parade, Cadet Nigel Butt, his white gloves gleaming, stepped up to receive the chief constable's baton as Cadet of the Year. Even his parents had to admit that he was a credit to the family.

Now unless something goes drastically wrong cadets normally make the transition into the regular force without difficulty. It's a question of investment of time and money. When Cadet Butt came up before the recruit selection board there were nods of approval all round. It was just a formality, a rubber stamp exercise. At the recruit training centre, Butt came consistently top of his class and when he was finally posted to S Division as a newly minted probationary constable, he had all the hallmarks of a model policeman. On his first morning the section sergeant read the glowing tributes on his file with a deepening scowl.

'Butt,' he began ominously, 'there's two things I can't abide. One's long haired hippy social workers and the others, cocky pro-cons. Now you've got your head stuffed full of all that book learnin' we're going to show you how to do some real police work and the first time you step out've line you're going to feel the toe of my boot . . . understand?'

The sergeant was a lean sparsely built ex-Royal Marine with a weathered face, expressionless eyes and a reputation as hard as a piece of cold steel, who despite the regulations still wore the buttons of the old Borough Force on his tunic. The sergeant was a 20-year veteran who strenuously resisted change. To him the station office was still the guard-room and his orders were to be obeyed, not questioned. He regarded himself and the other three stripers of the old guard still serving, as the backbone of a force which was going to the dogs, what with new fangled computers, pansy school liaison projects and the like. Among his pet hates were cadets who in his view somehow smacked of the 'officer and gentleman' system. Wet-nursing a bunch of nancy boys was no way to run a police force. And in his experience there was no better method of cooling down a young fireball like Nigel Butt than by teaming him with an old sweat like Ted Bogan. Thus, when he paraded the shift that morning, he ran through the briefing in his customary clipped military style, dispatched the panda patrols and the foot beats, then assigned PCs Bogan and Butt to the Sierra-Charlie-Four car.

Ted Bogan, a shambling bear in a shapeless uniform worn shiny at the seat and elbows, with his red face and bulbous blue veined nose, was an old time doorknob shaker whose unofficial duties included licking newcomers into shape.

'Son,' he told Butt as they climbed into their panda. 'Just so that we know where we stand right from the start, our job's lifting thieves, OK? All that sociology stuff they ram down your throats these days gives me bad indigestion.' He belched to emphasise the point and squinted at Butt: 'You didn't fall for any of that crap did you son?'

'I don't think so,' Butt replied tentatively. The last thing he wanted to do was to upset anyone on his first day and Bogan, he felt sure would be a formidable adversary.

'That's all right then,' Bogan seemed satisfied as he started the car and wheeled out of the station yard. 'One thing I can't stand is whining do-gooders. Our jobs nickin' 'em plain and simple, once you lose sight of that you might as well put your ticket in because you're not a copper any more.'

HO LEE
SWEET 8 SOUR
CHOW MEIN
EGG FOO YUNG
CHOP SUEY
FRIED RICE
FOO YIP
VAT INCL
CHIPS & FISH
MEGA BURGER
CURRY BUTTY
MUSHY PEAS
HE KNOWS NOWT ABOUT WOOD EITHER

Butt thought he might challenge Bogan's assertion and skilfully explode the myth of a policeman as avenger rather than social agent, but it was just a casual throwback to his studies which he dismissed almost immediately.

'And you don't make a good copper riding about in these bathtubs all day,' Bogan continued his lecture. 'A good copper works on his feet, not swanning around in a bloody car. That's why I always get you new kids so I can teach you some of the old craft of coppering before it's too late and the scum overrun us.'

Butt ventured to consider this remark somewhat high handed. What about the PNC, man-management and career motivation which had so obsessed the instructors at the training centre? He would also have liked Bogan to more clearly define the all-embracing expression 'scum'.

As though reading his mind Bogan said: 'Hammer 'em – that's what we're paid for and don't you forget that young Butt . . . hammer 'em.' Having issued this edict Bogan switched to a subject closer to his heart. 'Interested in DIY are you lad?'

Imagining this was some new abbreviation of police terminology which had so far eluded him Butt asked: 'DIY?'

'Do-it-yourself, son . . . do-it-yourself,' Bogan beamed, 'I'm a coffee table man . . . make a lovely job with a nice bit of pine though I say it myself. It's all in the wood you see . . .' He launched into a long rambling treatise comparing parana pine with Mexican hardwood and something called Jacinda oak; discussed the potential of variable speed electric drills and assorted gadgetry, talked lovingly of hardwoods and softwoods, crossgrains and sapele finishes, then just as bewilderingly switched the conversation again.

'Like Chinese?'

Butt considered the question, could discover no obvious pitfalls and so replied: 'I don't think I ever met any.'

'Food,' growled Bogan, 'Sweet and sour . . . crispy noodles . . . Foo Yung . . . spare rib . . .' He was salivating so heavily he had to stop.

'Oh yeah,' Butt replied, disappointed that the subject was

merely mundane and not some exciting insight into Triad lifestyles, 'I don't mind it.'

'Good.' Bogan took this as a favourable response. 'Nothing like Chinese nosh, puts hairs on your chest son.'

Over the following weeks it soon became apparent to Nigel Butt that whatever the duty scheme, Bogan's car had a roving commission on the sub-division and much of their time was spent either sampling Chinese delicacies at one or another of the restaurants and take-aways where Bogan was obviously a regular visitor, or ferreting about timber yards and handyman shops in pursuit of his hobby as an amateur carpenter. Eventually Butt saw through his partner's big crime fighter image. Whenever they were obliged to do some actual police duty, refereeing domestics and serving summonses seemed to be Bogan's best line of work. The only semblance of trouble came when they were called to a fight at a cafe and Butt, keying himself for the coming confrontation with violence, asked: 'Are we going in then Ted?'

'Shit NO.' Bogan looked horrified as he parked some distance from the cafe where the brawl had by then spilled out onto the pavement. 'Get on the blower and whistle up a Pixie.'

'A what?'

'Oh Christ!' Bogan grabbed the microphone and ignoring all radio procedure said: 'Hey sarge, get a Pixie down here right away OK. And about six blokes.'

Continuing his education into the subtleties of the job, Butt learned that night that the old black Maria or meat wagon was colloquially known as a Pixie as the first vehicle assigned to this role carried the registration letters PXE, and in the convoluted parlance of the Division was thereafter forever known as Pixie.

In fact as time wore on, Butt became aware of the fact that Bogan's aptitude for police work was singularly unenterprising. The day after Bogan had delivered him a lecture on the fallibility of Panda patrols in relation to the offence of shop-breaking . . . 'how in the name of Christ d'you ever think you're going to spot a jemmied lock or a busted window cruising your arse past at forty in a nice warm motor, I'll never know.' Bogan sniffed. 'See young Nigel, you've got to get out and wear down some shoe leather.'

They were on the night turn and Bogan demonstrated his theory by making Butt walk an entire shopping centre 'shaking door handles' while he sat in the darkened Panda parked in a side street nibbling sweet meat from a greasy bag full of spare ribs collected from one of his favourite Chinese haunts. Not that Butt minded. He was happy to get a breath of fresh air and escape from the Oriental odours which hung about in the police car for days on end.

But Bogan's skills as a tutor always seemed to fall short of the teach-by-example principle. When a break was reported at a radio and TV shop in the High Street, Bogan examined the door and then pronounced expertly: 'Two inch Cromwell number seven wood chisel. I'd stake me pension on it. No good for pine but it took this out clean as a whistle. Shoddy rubbish they're making door frames with these days . . . no craftsmanship.'

He took off his helmet, mopped his brow and then poked around inside the shop while Butt took some brief details from the owner.

'Look at that son,' Bogan called Butt into the rear store-room which had been systematically ransacked. He stirred what looked like orange pips with the toe of his shoe. 'That pip-spitter Billy Doyle's handiwork. Bastard never learns . . . always find his calling card if you look hard enough.'

Butt was impressed. 'Maybe we can nail him, eh Ted?' he asked eagerly.

'Hell no,' Bogan was adamant. 'That's a CID job . . . that's what they pay those jokers for, that and sitting on their backsides all day. You know what CID stands for . . . Coppers In Doors. You want to do their work as well? Jesus, you start that and the DI will fry your balls. Anyway, we've got more than we can cope with as it is.'

Even on the strength of their short acquaintanceship Nigel Butt was becoming mightily browned off with Ted Bogan. Finally he concluded that Bogan was nothing more than a fat lazy uniform-carrier, whose total knowledge of police work you could take between thumb and forefinger, sniff up your nose and it wouldn't even make you sneeze. But Nigel Butt reached this conclusion on the night of the Arrow Bridge jumper and by then it was too late.

The Arrow Bridge spanned the river just short of the docks where the grey water was pinched in a steep granite gorge and the span was at its narrowest. It was an ideal location according to the civil engineers who worked out the angles and the stress loads for the new suspension bridge which carried both road and rail across the river. With its gleaming white towers and curving cablework, the Arrow Bridge was a monument to advanced technology. A tribute to man's ingenuity. A civic landmark. A proud sentinel. And a royal pain in the neck for the police.

Almost from the moment the tape was cut and the traffic began to roll, freaks and exhibitionists, show-offs and potential suicides, flocked to the Arrow Bridge and, depending upon individual tastes, opted for the hundred and seventy foot drop from the sub-structure or added another hundred feet by scaling the suspension cables. The short drop was the favourite. All it required was throwing a leg over the parapet rail and shinning down to the latticework or girders which criss-crossed under the carriageway. But for the more ambitious, the challenge of the high wire act up there on the superstructure was too much to resist. Every one of them gave the police a king-sized headache.

Lately, whenever they worked the night turn, Bogan had taken to driving down to the bridge approach and just sitting in the parked Panda reminiscing about his days in the old Borough Force. At first Butt put this departure from usual routine of hopping from DIY emporium to Chinese restaurant, down to pure nostalgia. But even this illuminating little glimpse of Bogan's character was soon destroyed when Butt realised they always parked outside a small timber yard where they had once answered an arson call. Now a snatch of Bogan's conversation with the manager came back to him and slotted into place '. . . cheaper than Securicor . . .' and he remembered the lengths of prime timber which thereafter appeared mysteriously in the back of the Panda to be surreptitiously transferred to Bogan's private car back at the station. Whenever he raised the question of the bridge routine, Bogan would describe their nightly vigil as 'good old fashioned crime prevention,' adding, 'Show the flag son . . . that's what it's all about.'

But on this particular night Bogan's heart wasn't in it. It was a little after midnight and Butt detected a certain lack of enthusiasm when his partner's conversation deteriorated into a languid monologue on the merits of french polishing compared with polyeurathane varnish. He knew from experience that Bogan was itching to drive back into town to pick up a bag of deep fried crispy prawn and noodle rolls which were always on offer when the Hong Kong take-away closed down about 12.30. They had lapsed into deep reveries and the sudden rapping on the car window made they both jump in surprise.

Bogan wound down the glass and squinted out at a narrow frantic face.

'Thank God . . .' the man wheezed.

'What's your game pal?' Bogan began his customary challenge, but the man cut him short, gasping and puffing: 'The bridge!'

'What?'

'The bridge . . . the bridge!' The man began waving his arms.

'What about the bloody bridge?' Bogan was becoming rattled.

'The woman . . .'

'What woman?'

'On the bridge.'

'What?'

'I just seen her . . .'

'Hold on a minute . . .'

'. . . on the bridge . . .' The man was becoming hysterical as he tried to convey some sense of urgency, flailing the air with his arms and thumping the top of the police car. 'She's climbing up the cable!' He yelled into the policeman's face.

'Oh Christ,' Bogan groaned, and Nigel Butt leaned across to catch the drift, his face alive with excitement.

'Ted he's serious . . . we'd better take a look'.

'Oh no,' Bogan moaned in a low voice. 'I don't believe it . . . it can't happen to me.'

But Nigel had dissuaded the man from beating his tattoo on the car roof by hauling him inside where he calmed a little and offered to show them the way. Reluctantly, Bogan started the engine and began to roll slowly towards the bridge.

'Maybe you're seeing things pal,' Bogan tried hopefully as the man craned his neck this way and that, peering up into the night. 'Trick of the light . . . else you've had one over the eight and we're going to have to . . . .' But as they passed under the first tower the man yelled triumphantly: 'There!'

And as they got out of the car, peering upwards, they could just make out a pale blob against the black sky. 'There she is . . . I told you!' The man cried out again.

Even Bogan, head tilted back staring up at the diminutive figure high above them had to admit to himself: There's a jumper on the bridge all right. He began to curse softly under his breath, aware that Butt and the witness were watching him, expecting a decision. Eventually he seized Butt's elbow and drew him aside.

'Son,' he said, his shirt growing clammy as his sweat chilled in the crisp night air, 'looks like we've got a jumper up there.'

'What's the drill, Ted?' Butt asked in his usual eager fashion, but Bogan ignored him as he reached into the panda and unclipped the UHF. But when he tried to raise the station all he could get was a howl of static. Oh shit. Bogan was becoming rattled. He'd have to make the decision himself and as he looked around he could see a crowd was beginning to gather, people materialising from nowhere even at this Godforsaken time of night. Oh shit.

'Look Nigel,' he turned to Butt. 'I've got to call this in, it's my responsibility. You're going to have to go up there after her.'

Butt blinked in astonishment. He had expected something else, some well-oiled emergency plan to swing into operation. Special equipment, trained professionals moving surefootedly to the rescue. He hadn't imagined. . . .

'Look kid,' Bogan pressed on, 'I've got no choice. I'd go myself only . . .' he shrugged, suddenly tired of this charade '. . . only what the hell, I'm fat and I'm 50 and I get nosebleeds on a step ladder.'

'Can't we raise anybody?' Butt stammered, knowing full well that he would be gripped with vertigo and paralysed with fear the moment he even contemplated climbing up there.

'Nigel,' Bogan pronounced the Christian name with desperate emphasis. 'The radio's up the creek here. Jesus, you think I want to send you up there if I could avoid it? Only there's no way out son, we're stuck with it. There's people watching.' He swore viciously. 'Bastard jumpers . . . some stupid bitch!'

Butt's voice shook when he spoke. 'I don't know if I can do it Ted.'

'Come on kid', Bogan tried to sound confident. 'Just take it nice and easy, you'll be all right.'

'Ted . . . I don't think. . . .'

'I'll be back with the troops before you can bat an eyelid.'

'Ted. . . .'

'Dammit Nigel . . . you wanted to be a copper . . .' He thrust the flashlamp and a pocket radio into Butt's hand, ' . . . now's your chance to prove it.'

Before Butt could reply Bogan ducked inside the Panda, gunned the engine and squealed through a U-turn.

Nigel Butt watched the tail lights disappear and then with an awful sensation of loneliness, slowly crossed to the tower which reared up above him. The onlookers followed his progress with their eyes. The silence was absolute. Gulping air through his mouth to disguise the hammering of his heart, Butt tucked the torch into one pocket of his tunic, the radio in another, pulled his cap more tightly over his eyes and swung himself over the safety rail and onto the scaling ladder.

He climbed cautiously, gripping each rung so tightly that his knuckles ached, working his way up, hand over hand, never daring to look down. It was curiously easy, he discovered, using the ladders and catwalks provided for the maintenance crews and when he reached the cable, he was surprised at its size, like a great thick tree trunk arching away into the darkness. He could just make out the figure of the woman. She had gone some distance down the cable and had swung herself below it to perch on a cross spa with her legs dangling over the void. A solid wedge of fear thrust itself up into Butt's throat and threatened to choke him, but with a supreme effort he succeeded in persuading his limbs to respond and began to inch his way down the cable, wriggling forward, arms and legs wrapped around its rough steel girth. He had not gone far before he was gripped with a new sickening terror. The cable was moving!

Butt clung on for all he was worth as pain and fear vied for possession of his body. The superstructure of the bridge was not rigid as he had imagined it to be, it swayed slightly, taking and giving with the tolerances of its design. Perched there, 270 feet above the black water, Nigel Butt fought back wave after wave of nausea as he forced himself on.

'Come any closer and you're going to be the only one up here!'

The woman's voice floated up to him and with his face pressed against the cable he peered hesitantly around its curve and saw that he had almost reached her perch. A white oval face was just discernible in the darkness, looking up at him.

'Don't worry . . . don't worry . . .' he managed to stammer, 'I've . . . I've come to help . . . Oh God! The bile was rising in his throat and he knew he was going to be sick. 'I'm . . . I'm sorry . . .' he croaked, bitterly ashamed at his own weakness as he managed to remove his cap and threw up into it, retching uncontrollably.

'Oh boy,' the woman laughed at his plight. 'Young Sir Galahad . . . puking all over me. Here . . .' She reached up and took the cap from his trembling hand, '. . . you'd better give me that.' She hung the cap from a bolt head by its strap.

'I'm sorry,' Butt gasped as the heaving subsided. 'I can't . . . can't stand heights.'

The woman had moved closer, peering at him. 'Hey,' she said. 'You look like death.'

'I feel like it,' Butt confessed shakily.

'What're you doing up here anyway?'

'Police,' Butt managed. '. . . got to help you.'

'Oh God,' the woman said. 'That's what you get when you ask a stupid question.'

She regarded him for a few seconds longer and then said: 'You'd better come down here where I can see you . . . believe me you look awful.'

'I can't move.'

'Sure you can . . . here I'll help you.'

He felt her arms go around him as she guided him down to her perch on the spar where the two girders crossed.

'That's better,' she said, 'OK?'

Butt nodded. Fright had him in a powerful grip now and he couldn't trust himself to speak.

'Just relax,' the woman told him, 'listen have you got a cigarette?'

'I don't smoke,' Butt managed through chattering teeth and she laughed.

'Boy you're a lot of fun aren't you? And I just finished the packet too.'

'I'm sorry.'

'And stop saying you're sorry.'

'I'm sorry.'

'Oh Christ . . . where did they get you from? How old are you anyway?'

'Nineteen,' Butt said.

'Beautiful,' the woman said, 'That's all I needed . . . a teenage hero.'

'I want to help you,' Butt said, trying to control his faltering voice.

'*You* want to help ME?' The woman laughed again. 'You're sick, terrified, your teeth are chattering and you're cold as death and you want to help me! Nice try.'

'You don't understand . . . my job.'

'Look,' the woman said. 'If it'll make you feel better, my

life's a God-awful mess, I'm on sleepers and I'm on downers and I can't face myself in the mirror, so I came up here to do the only decent thing left and jump off the bloody bridge and I get landed with you.'

The thread of willpower which But had managed to salvage from his blind fear was beginning to wear thin. His vision was beginning to swim and he had already lost control of his bowels which appalled him.

'I think . . .' he began to sob. 'I think I'm going to pass out.'

'Oh no you don't,' she put her arms around him again and drew him close to her until he could feel the warmth of her body and then told him soothingly: 'This is my show little love – nobody cuts out on me, understand?'

As she continued to cradle his head he felt himself becoming calmer. 'What's your name?' he murmured, his cheek against her breast.

'Nancy,' she said 'Nancy Swain . . . how about you?'

'Nigel Butt,' he replied, his voice muffled by the fabric of her raincoat. 'Not that it's worth much right now. Pretty useless policeman aren't I?'

'Hey,' she said. 'Don't start coming that cop stuff again . . . Jesus I could murder a cigarette.'

'Why are you doing it Nancy?' Butt asked and Nancy Swain stroked his hair and said. 'Hush now. You don't want to hear Auntie Nancy's life story else you'll want to jump too. Let's just say there's a man I can't get out've my system who likes to tap dance on my face in hobnail boots every chance he gets and leave it like that, eh? It's like banging your head against the wall. Blissful when you stop.'

'I don't understand,' Butt said.

'Don't try,' her face was close to his. It was a plain face devoid of makeup with wide luminous eyes which were her most striking feature. A single woman passing through her late twenties with the certain knowledge that she wouldn't turn any heads in a crowd; with a desolate ache in her heart which gnawed at her mercilessly until she could bear it no longer. . . .

' . . . there's things in this life nobody should even have to understand. If you'd said to me last week, Nancy you're going to climb the old Arrow Bridge and take the high dive, I'd have laughed in your face and said you were crazy. Now here I am. There's things you just can't explain with words.'

'Nancy,' he gripped her tightly. 'Let me help you. . . .'

She continued to stroke his hair. 'You're a fine one to talk. How're you going to help me?'

'I don't know . . . there must be a way.'

'Phooey . . . they've all tried, the doctors, the trick-cyclists, I've been through the hoop so many times I could hand out a shingle.'

'D'you believe in God?'

'Oh sure . . . only he don't believe in me. Or if he does, he's got a funny way of showing it.'

There was a pause and then Nigel Butt could no longer suppress the selfish fear which reared uppermost in his mind. 'Please don't leave me here.'

She laughed. 'That's rich love. You come muscling in on my party and now you're laying down the law. I tell you what Nigel, wherever it is I get to, I'll send you a postcard. That's a promise.'

'Please . . .' Butt began to beg her brokenly, but his words cut off abruptly when a glaring white light washed over them as a powerful searchlight tracked the bridge. The radio, forgotten in Butt's pocket squawked into life.

'Chief Inspector Oswaldson to PC 492. Butt can you hear me? Are you all right?'

Stealing himself to look down, Nigel Butt saw far below the bridge was a hive of activity – police cars, fire engines, ambulances like miniature toys, the beams of the emergency lights probing the superstructure of the bridge. Panic seized him as the radio continued to demand his attention.

'Better give it to me,' Nancy Swain told him and he meekly handed over the set. She pressed the button. 'You down there! Switch off that bloody light else I'm bailing out right now!'

The light went out.

'That's better,' she said into the radio. 'Now listen to me, anybody tries to come up here the same applies, and I can see you coming a mile off . . . understand?'

'Who is this speaking?' the radio demanded.

'Never mind,' Nancy Swain replied wearily. 'Never mind.'

'Is PC Butt with you?'

'He's here.'

'Put him on then.'

'Get stuffed.'

'Now wait a minute . . .'

She placed the set beside her on the girder and sighed: 'God I need a cigarette.'

'Nancy,' Butt said, his face still pressed tightly against her. 'If you . . . if you go . . . I'm not going to make it.'

'Oh sure you will,' she replied soothingly. 'Trust me, trust Nancy. Hey do you remember that song, *Nancy with the laughing face* Sinatra? Well, I'm the other Nancy.' As she spoke the radio cracked again and the same voice said: 'Hey . . . on the bridge! PC Butt!'

Nancy Swain picked up the set again. 'Listen,' she said. 'listen carefully . . . are you getting this?'

'I can hear you,' the radio replied.

'Well I want you to know that PC Butt did everything he could. You got that?'

'Wait a minute,' the radio said. 'We're here to help you. Why don't you tell me your name and then. . . .'

But the appeal trailed off as with a deliberate flick of her wrist Nancy Swain sent the radio arcing out into the black night to fall to the river far below. Then she held Butt's face in her hands. 'Well this is it,' she said. 'They're going to be coming up any minute now. You just wait here Nigel and you'll be OK. Here, I'll make it easy.' She slipped the belt from her raincoat and looped it around the girder fastening the buckle. 'Hang onto this and don't let go until they get here. Got that?'

Tears were streaming down Butt's face. He was sobbing so hard that he couldn't speak.

She took his face in her hands again and kissed him on the lips, the salty taste of her own tears mingling with his. 'Come on now,' she said, her voice breaking for the first time, 'this is no way to say goodbye.'

Her legs were dangling over the void and she turned briefly, smiled and then tipped forward and Butt's tormented mind saw her as if in slow motion, recording the movement with all the dreadful lucidity of a cine camera winding down, frame by frame, until she was gone.

'Nancy!' he screamed her name until he was hoarse as he clung to the belt she had left him. 'NANCY!'

When they took Nigel Butt off the Arrow Bridge he was in shock. His eyes stared vacantly and his lips moved without sound. They kept the reporters and cameramen back beyond the barrier as they carried his stretcher through the harsh glare of the emergency lights. Chief Inspector Oswaldson, his fleshy face the colour of wax, walked alongside as they approached the ambulance.

'Looks all in don't he,' he told Bogan who was leaning against the open doors of the ambulance, perspiring profusely. 'I wonder what the hell happened up there.'

When the chief inspector turned away, Bogan leaned close to Butt's face and whispered: 'Come on son, snap out've it, you're missing all the glory. We could get commendations out've this.' But Nigel Butt merely stared back and showed no sign that he had even heard.

As luck would have it a spring tide was running that night and it was 10 days before they recovered Nancy Swain's body from the water, mangled and battered by the screws of the ships that plied the river. Just another job for the coroner. Nigel Butt had recovered by then from what his medical record euphemistically described as 'exposure and associated stress'.

The powers that be told him that only nutters jumped from the Arrow Bridge. Nutters like Nancy Swain . . . Nancy with the laughing face. Now that the inquest was over they told him to forget her and put the incident on the Arrow Bridge right out of his mind for his own good.

But he never would.

Five The Inspection

AT FIRST Deputy Chief Constable Henry Grey was convinced that the missing girl alert was just some stunt fabricated by the CID to impress the HMI. In his experience detectives were devious cunning characters who would stoop to the basest of trickery to promote a little special pleading. He was sick of hearing the constant moan of excessive case loads and escalating crime statistics to back up hysterical demands for extra CID manpower. Even when the girl's mutilated body was discovered, he still had a sneaking feeling that the whole sordid episode was simply an illusion created by the imagination of the Criminal Investigation Department. A little spanner in the works of the smooth inspection programme so that they could buttonhole the HMI with their bleatings about detective duty allowance, overtime allocations and subsistence rates. It was too much of a coincidence and it really was most inconsiderate.

'The trouble with crime,' said the HMI briskly, demonstrating his keen administrative grasp of the new topic of conversation. 'Is that you can never really trust it to play the game. Slippery customer, crime.'

They were taking luncheon in the mess and despite Grey's attempts to steer him off the subject, Sir Ralph Hawk seemed determined to talk about crime.

'Every time you build a new police station you get more crime because people have somewhere to go to report it. You could say that the whole police building programme is responsible for the rise in the crime rate.'

'Oh very droll Sir Ralph,' said Henry Grey, smiling appreciatively. 'I never though of it like that.'

'The trouble with crime Henry,' the HMI continued, 'is it's like quicksilver, always slipping through the old fingers. Damned elusive customer, crime.'

'Very true – very true,' Grey acknowledged the wisdom of the remark.

'You see,' said Sir Ralph Hawk, warming to the subject, 'When we talk about crime, we mean crime reported to the police. There's a whole lot of crime going on out there that we don't ever hear about. If everybody came running to us all the time with their problems, we'd have crime up to our ears Henry.'

'I suppose we would. . . .'

'There's no suppose about it,' said the HMI. 'And that's the trouble. Once you get the public all excited about crime, you're tinkering around with the tolerance levels and your crime rate is bound to go up. That gets people even more excited and you generate more and more crime.'

'So we need to keep the lid on the pressure cooker,' Grey voiced the notion which had come to him in a flash of inspiration.

Sir Ralph regarded him coolly. 'A mite too culinary for the analogy Henry, but reasonably close to the mark. The point I was making is the less said about crime – the better. Once you start working everybody up into a frenzy you just make the problems worse and end up in a vicious circle. Take juvenile crime for instance, everybody's in such an uproar about it. You know the only way to solve juvenile crime at a stroke Henry?'

Not wishing to make himself appear foolish, Grey merely shook his head politely.

'Raise the age of criminal responsibility to 17,' said Sir Ralph.

It took a moment for Grey to realise that the HMI was joking and by then it was too late. His own chuckle came as a hollow echo to Sir Ralph's laughter. 'Oh very droll Sir Ralph,' he added quickly, hoping to regain lost ground. 'That's a good one – I must remember that.'

Sir Ralph Hawk eased himself back in his chair, folded his snow white napkin and replaced it in a heavy silver serviette ring, one of the little touches of elegance for which Henry Grey prided himself.

'No, the damnable thing about crime is the myths it creates. Look at the detectives. This carefully fostered image of some sort of avenging angel is entire humbug. If the truth were known, the detective doesn't want to solve too much crime

...THEN WE DISBANDON THE DRUG SQUADS WHICH IN TURN SOLVES THE DRUG PROBLEM, THEN...

otherwise he's out of business. Has it ever occurred to you Henry, that detectives have a vested interest in keeping the crime rate up. It's their raw material, the stuff myths are made of.'

'Oh I agree Sir Ralph,' Grey replied enthusiastically.

'In fact,' the HMI pressed on with his hypothesis, 'you could say that the detective is the last person you should entrust with crime. He's far too personally involved to take a dispassionate viewpoint.'

'My sentiments entirely,' Grey said. 'You put it so well Sir Ralph.'

'Hmmm . . .' the HMI mused, 'It's an interesting proposition, might take a look at one or two detectives while I'm here Henry, see how they shape up. . . .'

Six Detectives

'IT'S impossible,' Dennis Jewel said, without taking the pipe out of his mouth so that the words came out strangled. 'Even if you'd got a *case* of Black Label tucked under your arm there I'd be telling you the same thing.'

Brian Webber placed the bottle of whiskey he had brought along as a sweetener, on the desk between them. 'Dennis,' he said, 'what say you lock the door there, we pull a couple of glasses out've your bottom drawer and we sip a little of this stuff and see if you don't change your mind.'

'There's no way I'm going to do that,' Jewel replied, still talking around the stem of his Peterson, 'not while we've got an operation running. You think I can conjure blokes up out've the air or something? I'm not a bloody magician, Brian.'

Webber sighed. He'd come to the crime squad for a favour and he'd expected to have a wrangle, but here was Jewel sitting on his backside just acting stubborn. 'What operation?'

'Zatopek – you know, the antiques thing.'

'Zatopek?'

'Don't you start,' Jewel took the pipe from his mouth and began to scour out the bowl into an ashtray. 'Some comedian up country came up with that stupid name, something about it going to run the distance. . .'

'Christ,' Webber said. 'Now I've heard everything.'

'Well it don't change anything,' Jewel insisted, refilling his pipe. 'I'm committed a hundred per cent and if they get wind up the road that I'm even *thinking* of loaning blokes to you on the old pals act, they're going to have my balls, it's as simple as that.'

Brian Webber regarded his friend for a long moment as he marshalled his thoughts for the next assault. Jewel was a heavily built man, solid with beefy shoulders which bulged under his shirt. He had a head of tight grey curls and his face wore a permanently perplexed expression. They were the same rank, detective chief inspector, only Jewel was seconded to the local office of the regional crime squad which was independent of the force and had its own complement of detectives. He took his orders from a district co-ordinator who oversaw the work of the branch offices of the No. 12 squad in different forces. Normally the regional crime squad would be only too happy to oblige on tricky investigations which stretched the limited resources of the local CID, but now that Webber wanted that help, here was Dennis Jewel belly-aching about some Zatopek thing. Jewel had his pipe relit before Webber tried a different tack.

'Look Dennis, it's not like I'm asking for the earth, just a couple of decent blokes would do. As it is I'm really right up against it, I've got the circus from headquarters around my neck, the boss already shouting the odds on overtime and a week-old murder we've only just come in on.'

'Yeah, I see your problem,' Jewel agreed. 'You've got cold meat there all right Brian. Not many like that get cleared these days.'

'That's what I like about you Dennis – always an optimist.'

'Well you've got to be a realist sometimes,' Jewel said, 'sounds like it's all stacked against you. If I was you Brian, I'd think seriously about coasting and leave those eager beavers from headquarters to take the shit when it all folds up on 'em.'

'Come off it,' Webber said. 'You never took a soft option in your life and I'm the same. We're a couple of thick-skinned D's who happen to think clearing crime still matters, particularly a swine like this one. That's what I pin my reputation on, not ducking and diving and playing politics. And don't try to kid me you're not the same.'

Jewel shrugged. 'You don't get any medals for pissing into the wind these days.'

'I'm talking about in here,' Webber tapped his chest. 'Personal satisfaction Dennis, professional pride, call it what you like. And I'm buggered if I'm going to let some lunatic who'd stick a screwdriver into a kid like that 'till she looked like a colander get away with it. If I started back peddling this one I wouldn't sleep nights – and you know it.'

Jewel heaved his shoulders again: 'All you'll get yourself's an ulcer Brian.' He puffed on his pipe then said: 'I tell you

I'LL LEND YOU A COUPLE OF THESE BRIAN, THEY ARE BETTER THAN THE REAL DETECTIVES
STANDBY SQU

what, run through it for me and maybe something'll come to mind. What've you got so far?'

'Well first off we've got the car, beat-up Cortina, we found her in the boot. There's a lot of blood in there and in the back of the car, and the back seats are missing, so that's where it could've happened. The doc says she was dead best part of five days, so matey's got a head start.'

'How about the car. Any good?

Webber pulled a face. 'You'd have thought so, wouldn't you? We got the owner right away and put him through the mincer. His story is he's away on holiday and he's left the car in the street outside his home and somebody must've nicked it because the first he knows is he comes home and there's the law beating down his door.'

'Sounds like a good story for the spur of the moment. How's it stand up?'

'That's the trouble,' Webber said. 'It's cast iron and watertight. He's got about a thousand witnesses backing up his alibi and we can't shake 'em. Looks like he's telling the truth or else he's got a lot of clout somewhere to rig a thing like that.'

'What's he like?

'A charmer.' Webber said. 'Form for rape and indecent assault. Complaints against the police for pastime. A right charmer. If his story wasn't so rock solid he'd be right there in the frame. I'd 'ave had him strung up by his thumbs by now.'

'That's the way it goes.' Jewel said. 'How about associates. Maybe he's got some pals of similar persuasion. Maybe he loaned somebody his motor.'

'Well if he did,' Webber replied, 'he's not going to be telling us about it. He's as cunning as a barrel-load of monkeys, so we're not going to be able to pull any flankers with him otherwise there'll be white forms coming down like a blizzard.'

'What else you got?'

'What would you like?' Webber asked. 'We only got onto the job yesterday. Oh we've got a few possible witnesses only now the brass've arrived, stirring it up, everybody's leaping about like blue arsed flies trying to put on a big show of keen dedicated CID work everybody'll remember come the next promotion board. Every bugger's so busy hustling his image, I can see this job going right out've the window.'

'Don't take it so personally,' Jewel counselled, 'you're going to lose your objectivity.'

'Advice like that I can do without. Now are you going to take that incinerator out've your face and give me some help on this or not?'

'I'd like to,' Jewel softened a little, gazing reflectively at his pipe. 'Only I can't see any way I could squeeze it without some bright bugger noticing.'

'Just one decent D'd do me,' Webber said. 'All my blokes have been yanked off in every direction. I just need somebody to watch my back.'

'One D,' Jewel tapped his teeth with the stem of his pipe and contemplated the ceiling.

'At a pinch – yes.'

'I tell you what,' Jewel lowered his gaze and there was a hint of a smile on his lips. 'I could maybe loan you Helen Ritchie. . . .'

'What!'

'Come on, Helen's a bloody good detective. You ought to know that Brian.'

'Oh Christ, Dennis – that's below the belt.'

'Best I can do.' Jewel was grinning openly now. 'Take it or leave it – d'you want her or not?'

Webber groaned. 'I've got no choice have I?'

'Nope.'

Webber reached across the desk and retrieved the bottle of whiskey. 'For a low trick like that you don't deserve my hospitality.'

'That's all right,' Jewel was amused at his friend's obvious discomfort. 'I switched to gin anyway. Smoother on the old tubes.'

Webber gazed reflectively at his amber reflection in the bottle. 'How is Helen anyway – I haven't seen her in years?'

'How d'you mean?' Jewel asked, puffing contentedly, eyes twinkling nonchalantly. 'Jobwise or what?'

'You know what I mean Dennis,' Webber said. 'How the hell is she?'

'Well . . .' Jewel said. 'I always got the feeling something must've soured Helen way back. Oh, she still looks terrific, but inside . . . Well . . . who knows what goes on inside their heads. These days Helen's got this women's lib thing round her neck, you only have to look at her sideways and she's up there on her high horse. I always got the impression that somewhere along the line some smooth talking bastard slipped something nasty up her roll-on and she's never got over it. I heard she was a really sweet kid back along before I came to the squad.' Jewel took the pipe out of his mouth and began to excavate the bowl again. 'But you'd know better'n me Brian . . . you were on the squad with her in those long gone days, weren't you?'

'Sure,' Webber said, picking up his bottle and preparing to leave, 'back when we were young and impressionable and everybody was breaking their neck to prove what a great D they were.'

'Good times, eh?' Jewel said. 'So who d'you think slipped Helen a crippler?'

'How would I know?,' Webber said, 'I was only with the squad six months, then I got moved to C11 at the Yard and I was out've circulation for a couple of years.'

'Oh yeah, I recall,' Jewel said. 'You were a flier in those days, eh Brian. We used to sit here chewing on our straws and watching your career take off. First the Yard, then the College and all that clever stuff. You were the blue-eyed boy then, Brian.'

'Didn't last long though, did it?'

'Oh come on,' Jewel blew down the stem of his pipe to complete the cleaning process. 'Don't tell me you're getting bitter and twisted too.'

Webber crossed to the door and Jewel followed him with his eyes.

'So how about Helen – d'you want her or not?'

'I'll let you know.' Webber said as he went out.

* * *

Marian was putting the kids to bed, he knew that by the familiar noises in the rooms below him. Brian Webber sat at the little kneehole desk he had picked up cheap at an auction, in the spare bedroom which served as his study. There was no other suitable room in the standard semi-detached house the force provided him with rent-free.

It was after 8 o'clock when he got home from the station and he was tired to the point of exhaustion. He'd told his wife that all he needed was a few minutes' peace and quiet and he'd gone up to his study, taking the bottle of whiskey with him. And for no good reason he'd broken the seal and poured himself a drink. He nursed the glass for a moment, reflecting upon his thickening waist, the product of too many beers, too many snatched sandwich lunches, the unmistakable evidence of approaching middle age, then swallowed the whiskey in one gulp. He poured himself another. It was unusual for him to act in this way. Normally he would never shut himself away from his family, he had precious little time with them anyway. Neither would he dream of drinking alone, but then tonight was different. Tonight he was fortifying himself against a deep melancholy as his memory conjured up images from the past, images of Helen Ritchie.

Had 12 years really slipped past like the blink of an eyelid? All these years had she really dwelt somewhere deep in his memory, waiting for the right moment to return and torment him. Brian Webber massaged his eyes with thumb and forefinger, then pinched the bridge of his nose. It all seemed like yesterday.

* * *

It was back in the heady days of the mid-sixties when Brian Webber, billeted in single men's quarters, began to get the feeling a bright young man could make a name for himself in the police force. The old adage 'in the country of the blind, the one-eyed man is king' seemed more and more appropriate as he assauged his sexual appetite on an ample diet of nurses and manoeuvred himself into the CID. It was a time of plenty.

A time of golden opportunity. A time when rose tinted dreams came true, and for Brian Webber breathing the sweet clean air of ambition, promotion to detective sergeant in record time came as a natural reward for his talents. Within a month he had engineered himself a transfer to the regional crime squad; had moved into a stylish bachelor flat and was driving an MG sports car.

His star was well and truly in ascendance. The squad appealed to his vanity, the swashbuckling image of the elite crime fighter, the absence of regimented routine. He began to affect the sharp mohair suit, allowed his hair to grow a little longer than regulations permitted, adopted the vernacular of the squad which was heavily laced with Metropolitan jargon. Brash, flashy, aggressive and conceited, that was the veneer and it pleased him to discover that when he went into a bar for a quiet drink, a proportion of the patrons would slink away in the direction of the rear exit. In his own impressionable eyes, Brian Webber was a 'bloody good D' who put the fear of God into the criminal fraternity. So when a policewoman named Helen Ritchie joined the squad for a plain clothes attachment, it seemed only natural in the incestuous world of the police that an affair was on the cards.

Helen Ritchie was a doll, no two ways about it, and plainly, she had been selected for the squad because she bore not the slightest resemblance to the archetype policewoman. She was small, fine featured with a model's figure and a walk with pelvis thrust forward which brought a chorus of wolf whistles from building sites. She wore her coppery hair in a mass of finger curls like a burnished halo around her elfin face. Even her nose wrinkled delightfully when she smiled.

Her first day on the squad produced a desperate race to see who could tempt her out to lunch. Brian Webber won by a long head. Pretty soon they were seen out regularly together; driving out into the country to watch sunsets from the parked MG; taking long walks hand in hand, kissing lightly and entwining fingertips. After a surfeit of nurses, Brian Webber was enchanted by Helen Ritchie, felt a fluttering sensation inside himself whenever they were together, a mild anxiety when they were apart. It was a unique experience. Times when he lay on the settee in his flat her head cradled in his lap, awash with the romantic imagery of the latest Andy Williams' album.

'Helen.'

'Hmm.'

'I love you.'

'U–huh.'

'I really do.'

'What?'

'Love you.'

'Oh yeah?'

'Come on – I'm serious.'

'All right.' Her eyes were closed as she listened to the music.

'I really love you.'

'How d'you know?'

'What?'

'How d'you know you love me?'

'I just feel it.'

'How d'you feel?'

'Oh – come on.'

'Brian,' she said, opening her eyes and smiling when she said it. 'What makes you think you love me?'

'I just know it.'

'You *think* you love me. We'd need a lot more time before you'd know it.'

'Oh come on Helen.'

'Believe me Brian, you love yourself more than you love me – when that changes, *I'll* know it.'

'That's a pretty cruel thing to say.'

'There's no sense in kidding ourselves, give it time, don't rush it.'

'But I love you *now*.'

She closed her eyes. 'Relax Brian, listen to the music.'

Times like this, he thought to himself, she could be infuriating, but he swallowed his injured pride and tried to imagine what it would need to really convince her. He had no way of knowing of course that the convoluted process of female courtship required edging forward slowly, consolidating each move before surrendering further resources of emotion. He had no way of knowing that Helen was already enmeshed in the complicated emotional tangle of her gender that he had unleashed within her. His feelings were still too shallow for that kind of comprehension and Helen Ritchie, playing the game dictated by her instincts would certainly never admit it. As if that wasn't enough, sometimes the job intruded.

They were driving home from a restaurant when Helen who had been in a pensive mood all evening said: 'Let's just park over there Brian and talk a minute.'

Webber drew the MG into a layby overlooking a wooded valley. It was a warm summer evening and the tranquillity of the surrounding countryside compounded their reflective mood. Webber switched off the engine and they sat for a moment in absolute silence.

'Penny for 'em then?'

Helen turned to face him: 'How serious is withholding information?'

Webber was taken aback. 'How d'you mean?'

'In the job.'

'Depends.'

She bit her lip. 'I mean d'you switch off when you're off duty, Brian. Can you have a personal life as well?'

Webber smiled. 'Like the Pinkertons, we never sleep.'

'Brian I'm serious.'

'Well,' he said, 'you know the score as well as I do Helen, particularly with the squad, a good D's supposed to put the job first.'

'What about us?'

Webber shrugged; 'We've done all right so far, there's no regulation says you can't live your own life. What's the problem anyway?'

Helen was staring out of the car window. 'How important is Bernard Goodman?' she asked softly.

Webber jerked upright in his seat. 'What d'you know about Bernard Goodman?'

'Only that he's a squad target.'

'Jesus, that's the understatement of the year. The number nine have been busting a gut over him for six months or more.'

'Big deal then eh?'

'Helen.' Webber said. 'Bernard Goodman ripped off two hundred grand from the London headquarters of the Bank of Japan. He's not just big deal, he's number one ace.'

'I'm the new girl.' Helen said, still without looking at him. 'Tell me what makes him so special?'

'Look love – Bernie's the best lance man in the business. He went through the vault of that bank like butter. Went in from an old warehouse across the street with ducting and fans to take away all the smoke. Bernie's magic with a thermic lance. The Met's never got a sniff on that job.'

'I know where he is.'

Webber was stunned. 'Say that again.'

'I know where he is Brian.' She turned to face him, her expression sombre.

'You're kidding.'

She shook her head. 'I wish I was.'

Webber took her hand in his. 'Look Helen,' he said carefully, 'this is serious. Are you telling me you know where Bernie Goodman is – right now, this minute?'

She nodded.

'Jesus Christ.' Webber breathed. 'You'd better tell me about it love.'

'It's not that simple.'

'Look Helen – we're not talking about some cheapskate villain you know, Goodman's a squad target. Any D worth his salt'd give his eye teeth to nail him. That's the sort of stuff reputations are made of.'

'I know,' she said, 'that's what worries me.'

'Love,' Webber said, still holding her hand in his, 'if you know anything about Bernie Goodman, you'd better tell me about it.'

'As you and me – or as detectives?'

'As you and me – God if we can't trust each other now it's a poor lookout.'

'All right,' she agreed. 'Its funny how it happened. I mean *me* getting the whisper on a thing like this.'

'Go on – tell me about it.'

Helen frowned. 'Well when I was doing my initial training at Ryton there was a girl in my class called Carol Dunne. How she ever got into the job I'll never know, you could see a mile off she'd never make it. Anyway, I felt sorry for her and we became friends. Weekends I used to go and stay with her family in the Cotswolds. She was a strange girl and I always got the feeling she'd joined the police in desperation to try to bring some sort or order into her life. But it didn't work and after Ryton she only did a couple of months in the job then packed it in. We kept in touch for a while and then she drifted to London and started working as a croupier in the clubs. It could have been reaction from the boredom of trying to settle down, something of the sort. Then after a bit I didn't hear from her again and I thought she'd broken all her old ties one by one and I was the last. Anyway a couple of years went by and I didn't hear from her, then last week, right out of the blue she 'phoned me and said she wanted to see me about something important, something she wouldn't talk about on the 'phone. She sounded so desperate I agreed to meet her, but you know if she hadn't made the first move I'd never have recognised her. She'd changed completely, looked like a real hard faced little bitch.' Helen paused for a moment and then continued: 'Well to cut a long story short, she told me she was living with this Greek and working nights as a croupier and hostess at the Desert Island Club. She said this boyfriend of hers was a right charmer who'd get juiced up and knock her about then plead with her and come crawling back when he was dried out again. Said she stuck with him because he needed her. . . .'

'The Desert Island,' Webber interrupted, 'that's Danny Hood's place, he's a real nutter, had the whole place fitted out in sand coloured carpet, with footprints all over it. Must've cost a bomb. Used to be a pretty fair heavyweight boxer before he got punchy and drifted into bad company.'

'Well anyway,' Helen continued. 'Carol told me she was terrified because this boyfriend of hers has got in over his head with Hood. So I told her I couldn't help her unless she was more specific and she came right out with it. She told me they've got Goodman locked up in a back room at the club and they're squeezing him dry. She said the deal had started off as a hideout, but now he was a prisoner and the thing was getting out of hand.'

Webber was suspicious: 'How'd she know all this?'

'Apparently the Greek's inclined to brag when he's got a few under his belt and she's scared stiff they're going to find out and do something to keep him quiet.'

'Well she knows the score there all right,' Webber said, 'that's about Hoods's barrow.'

'She said she couldn't think of any way out, then she remembered me.'

'OK Helen,' Webber was sceptical. 'So she comes to you and spins you this yarn. What's to say it's not just some fairy story she's dreamed up. What's her angle?'

'There's a kid.' Helen said. 'She's had a baby by the Greek, and I finally got it out of her, that's what's eating her up. One of our little feminine quirks.'

'OK,' Webber said. 'You get her to come in and we can put something together. We're going to need a warrant and that means reasonable grounds, so we need something – a picture would do. D'you think she could handle a camera. . . .'

'Brian,' Helen said. 'You haven't understood a word I've said to you. There's no way Carol can be involved or me either. What d'you think I was talking to you about withholding evidence for?'

'Look love – on a thing like this we'll give her protection around the clock and you're a squad officer anyway, you don't have a choice.'

'No way,' Helen insisted. 'That bunch of maniacs would connect me to Carol right away and she'd be in worse trouble than she is now. We can't look after her forever.'

'I could go to the guvnor, lay it on the line. . .'

'Oh Brian, then I'd have to deny this conversation ever took place. Don't you see? She's put me in an impossible position, besides, I feel responsible for her. We were good friends once.'

She looked so crestfallen that Webber took her face in his hands and kissed her lightly. 'Well you got it off your chest love, that's a good thing. Now you leave it to me, I'll work something out.'

But the prize of Bernie Goodman, ace one target, was too much to resist. The following morning Webber called his team together for a little conference. He laid it on the line for them without disclosing his source of information.

'The only way around this,' he told them, 'is to take that pillock Dan Hood out've the frame and soften him up a bit – then we'll collect Goodman.'

'Nick him official skip?' one of the DCs asked and Webber shook his head.

'No – this one's a foreigner, we'll do it off our own bat and see how it shapes up. We'll book out on general observation tonight and rendezvous on the car park of the Black Horse. Two cars'll do – oh and one of you sign for a shooter, give 'em the usual rigmarole, OK?'

Working to Brian Webber's instructions they picked up Daniel Hood that night, sandwiching his pink Ford Galaxie between the police cars as he drove away from the Desert Island Club shortly after midnight. The exchange in the street was brief and to the point. After forcing the gaudy American convertible to a halt the armed detective thrust a short barrelled .38 through the driver's window into the neck of the bodyguard behind the wheel, whose eyes immediately took on a glazed and far-away look. Webber opened the passenger door and told Hood: 'Don't even breathe Danny, you're the star turn for tonight.'

They took Hood directly to the central mortuary just as Webber had planned. In the austere clinical surroundings which reeked of death and disinfectant, they ordered him to strip naked and then laid him out on one of the freezer drawers which had been rolled out for the purpose.

Daniel Hood was a hard man. He had a hard smooth face drawn taut by scar tissue, a legacy of his days in the ring. His huge body had begun to run to fat and looked strangely vulnerable stretched out in the drawer. His cold eyes regarded the detectives speculativley and betrayed no emotion. Daniel Hood was accustomed to playing games with the squad.

Brian Webber, mohair sleek under the harsh neon light, twisted a toe tag around his finger. 'Heard you've got a lodger down the Island these days Danny.'

'What makes you think that Mr Webber?'

'Just a whisper, Danny.'

'Someone's pulling your leg Mr. Webber.'

'Name of Bernie Goodman.'

'Bernie Goodman? Never heard of him.'

'And he's outstayed his welcome Danny.'

'I don't know where you get 'em from Mr Webber.'

Webber gave the drawer a shove and it slid back into the freezer with a whirr of rollers. He waited a moment and then rolled Hood out again.

'About this lodger of yours Danny.'

Hood's teeth chattered when he spoke. 'I already told you. I don't know what you're talking about.'

'You'll remember in a minute or two Danny.' Webber said and he repeated the treatment wheeling Hood in and out of the freezer. His teeth were clenched now, his lips turning blue, but the eyes remained expressionless.

'See – the way we reckon it Danny,' Webber told him, 'Is you've had your pound of flesh out've old Bernie, now it's our turn. So how about it?'

'Get stuffed copper,' Hood replied flatly.

The interrogation followed the same pattern for a while longer with the drawer carrying Hood in and out of the freezer like a yo-yo. Finally when Hood could no longer feel his extremities, he began to relent.

'This cock and bull story of yours Mr Webber – supposing it was true. I'd be daft to admit it without some safeguards, wouldn't I?'

'We're not interested in you Danny,' Webber reassured him, 'you know our motto, always save something for another day. You're not due yet.'

'So what's in it for me?'

'Insurance Danny.'

'Come again.'

'You play ball with us and we won't tell Bernie's little firm what a diabolical stroke you've been pulling with their best mate. Because if we did that . . .' Webber took the tag and tied it to Hood's big toe '. . . might have to make you a permanant reservation.'

'Who put the bubble in?'

'Be your age Danny.'

Hood breathed a sigh. 'All right you've got me cold.'

Webber smiled down at him: 'More like on ice,' he said.

The crime squad hit the Desert Island club mob-handed at five o'clock that morning and lifted Bernard Goodman clean as a whistle. It was a textbook operation.

'You should've seen the poor bugger,' Webber told his DI when they returned to the office. 'Squatting there in his underpants and blubbering like a baby. A few more days of that kind of medicine and he'd have been a goner.'

'You got a good snout on that one all right Brian,' the DI told him admiringly. 'Do you a bit of good too.'

Webber shrugged: 'Good intelligence,' he replied, 'could have happened to anyone.'

'Pull the other one,' the DI said. 'The guvnor's delighted with you – a real feather in your cap. You could be going places after this.'

Basking in the glory of the moment Brian Webber went back to his flat to freshen up and change his clothes. It was his big chance for he was to lead the escort taking Goodman back to London and he had heard on the grapevine that the commander of C11 at the Yard was showing interest. The 'phone was ringing.

'Quite the little hero, aren't we?' It was Helen's voice, sharp and brittle.

'Helen!' Webber exclaimed. 'I was going to call you . . it worked like a dream. . I'm just off to hand him over to the Met,' he glanced at his watch, saw that time was slipping away. 'Look love, I've got to dash. . . .'

'You bastard Brian.' The words cut through him like a knife. 'You rotten bastard.' Her voice broke a little with pent up emotion. 'I just had to call from the Accident Hospital. They brought Carol in DOA, hit and run accident. She came out've her flat, went to cross the road and wham!! Does that make you feel proud of yourself, you bastard!'

Webber gripped the 'phone in disbelief. 'Helen,' he said, 'listen – I didn't. . . .'

'You really take the prize Brian.' She was crying now. 'You know that? You killed her as sure as if you'd done it yourself, you bastard. You'd stiff your own mother for a pat on the head.'

'Helen, listen to me. . . .'

'And you know what? She was carrying a note in her pocket saying to call me in case of accident, how's that for a laugh!'

'Hey Helen, you don't think I had anything to do with that,' Webber exclaimed desperately. 'I never even mentioned her name – or yours either. I kept you both out've it, you've got to believe that. Helen? Helen love?' But he was talking to the dialling tone.

Webber stared at the 'phone for a moment, his thoughts in a turmoil. It must have been a coincidence, a quirk of fate. He considered calling the traffic officers and asking for details of the accident that had killed Carol Dunne, contemplated going immediately to Helen and somehow convincing her that he had not broken his word. He consulted his watch again. There just wasn't time.

And so Brian Webber went to London with his prisoner, seized his chance with both hands and was whisked off the squad for a sojourn at the Yard. It was the sort of opportunity any ambitious detective would have happily cut off an arm for. Helen Ritchie was expendable.

* * *

Now, sitting in his makeshift study reflecting upon a glass of whiskey, with the benefit of hindsight Brian Webber knew it had all been a charade and that his early promise had burned out like a shooting star. Had the guilt which gnawed within him for turning his back on Helen's tragic outburst eventually eaten him away? Was that the answer? At moments like this he would concede that possibility. At moments like this he would sacrifice his comfortable domesticity, his career, everything, for the chance to roll back the years and make Helen Ritchie understand that he had no hand in Carol Dunne's death.

His wife was calling from downstairs and it was time to cap the bottle and put aside such maudlin thoughts. He had responsibilities and he had to live with them. That was the hard lesson of reality – never look back. In the morning he would call Dennis Jewel and tell him to forget it.

Seven The Inspection

'HEARD of silicon law Henry?' Sir Ralph Hawk inquired as they travelled between police stations in the staff car.

Henry Grey's smooth brow furrowed slightly. 'Was it mentioned in ACPO circulars, Sir Ralph? I try to keep up to date with the circulars, but I don't recall . . .' His voice trailed off.

'Too hush-hush for ACPO,' the HMI chided gently. 'Top drawer stuff really. Need to know only, that sort of thing.' He turned a quizzical eye on the deputy chief. 'Your PV's current of course Henry?'

From any lesser personage Henry Grey would have taken that query as a grave affront. He was a stickler for Positive Vetting. 'Naturally Sir Ralph,' he replied, a little tartly.

'You can never be too careful when it comes to security,' the HMI said. 'Neglect your security and you're courting trouble.'

'I make a point of it,' Grey replied, 'you won't find a more security conscious force than this one, not by a long chalk.'

'Glad to hear it,' said Sir Ralph Hawk. 'Can't say the same for ACPO though, some rum types slipping through the net these days.'

It intrigued Grey to hear Sir Ralph's implied criticism of the Association of Chief Police Officers to which every senior rank from assistant chief upwards belonged. He had vaguely formed the opinion himself that standards were slipping of late. Why at the last conference he'd even spotted an ACC wearing a corduroy suit and suede shoes.

'Well as I was saying,' the HMI returned to his original theme. 'Silicon law's pretty hot stuff. Got everybody excited at the Home Office.'

'That's very interesting Sir Ralph,' Grey said, pricking up his ears at the mention of the Home Office.

'You've got to hand it to the backroom boys in the research unit, they're hot as mustard.'

'I'm the soul of discretion Sir Ralph,' Grey assured him, beside himself now with curiosity. 'Whatever you say to me goes no further.'

'Well . . .' the HMI deliberated. 'Strickly entre nous then Henry. . . .'

'Oh of course Sir Ralph.'

'Funny how it happened really,' Sir Ralph mused. 'I gather a bunch of bright sparks were sitting around one day wondering how they could spend some money. Apparently there was a shortfall on the research budget, then someone just came up with ACE right out of the blue.'

'ACE Sir Ralph?'

'Automatic Computer Enforcement,' the HMI explained. 'That's the official title of the project only those in the know call it silicon law. All part of the jargon.'

'How interesting.'

'Oh it's fascinating. You see this silicon chip thing means you can get a computer the size of a double decker bus down to a pinhead. I don't pretend to understand how it's done – leave all that to the scientist chaps. Fine brains, you know Henry, fine brains.'

'I know Sir Ralph – first rate fellows.'

'Well they thought if you could implant one of these pinhead gizmos into a person's central nervous system, all sorts of possibilities opened up.'

'You couldn't do that with a double decker bus,' Henry Grey observed, marvelling at the advance of science.

'Quite so,' said Sir Ralph Hawk. 'But the really tremendous advance, is if you can do that, it's feasible that you could control criminal tendencies.'

'Good Lord!' Henry Grey exclaimed.

'The theory being,' said the HMI, 'that you could have a centralised computer linked into all these tiny implants and whenever anybody was even thinking of breaking the law, the computer would send out an instant punishment impulse automatically. All that you'd need is to keep the programming up to date with current legislation.'

'Good Lord,' Henry Grey repeated, dazzled by the prospect.

'And hey presto,' said the HMI, 'You've got ACE, automatic computer enforcement.'

WEST BANK
LONDON BUS

The deputy chief tried to get to grips with the enormity of the suggestion. 'But tell me Sir Ralph,' he said, 'how would the main computer keep in touch with all these implants. Wouldn't people be trailing all sorts of wires around. . . .'

The HMI laughed out loud. 'You're even more old fashioned than I am Henry, haven't you heard of light waves and laser beams and parked orbit communications satellites?'

'I'm still trying to grasp the double decker bus on a pinhead,' admitted Henry Grey glumly.

'Well take it from me, the backroom boys have got it all taped. There'll be a few politicians hanging their hats on ACE before too long, you mark my words.'

'How will they manage to implant these . . . er . . . pinheads, Sir Ralph. I mean – there'd be one hell of a stink. . . . '

'It'd be phased in,' the HMI said, 'low profile, you couldn't rush it.'

'Those NCCL jokers would go berserk.'

'Then we'd implant them first,' said the HMI logically.

'But wouldn't it be a denial of liberty, everything we stand for. . . . '

'You don't approve of people breaking the law do you?' replied the HMI testily.

'Oh no, Sir Ralph,' Grey hastened to add.

'I should hope not. No – you must learn to take the broader view Henry, technology's here to stay whether we like it or not.'

'Sir Ralph, please believe me, I didn't mean . . . .'

'I'm sure you didn't Henry. Personally I don't think silicon law's any more of an intrusion on liberty than bleeding us white through direct taxation. But that's beside the point. What interests me Henry, is the impact on the service.'

'How d'you mean Sir Ralph?'

'Well think it through man. If you've got Automatic Computer Enforcement, you're not going to need policemen any more. We'd be extinct Henry, extinct as the dinosaur. . . .'

Eight Bishop's Waistcoat

THE waistcoat was Bob Bishop's trademark. It was made of the brightest red tie silk, vivid scarlet which flashed whenever he unbuttoned his jacket. And just lately the name and the waistcoat had become synonymous so that whenever either one was mentioned within the cloistered company of the S Division, there was much cursing and tearing of hair. For they evoked fear and hatred in generous proportions. They were the tangible evidence of an aberration of the system to which they all paid unswerving allegiance; the clawing, connivance, ulcer-ridden scramble for promotion. It was even suggested that the chief constable himself, would sometimes quake in his shoes whenever mention was made of his brainchild. Not that anyone had been able to verify such a portentous rumour because these days the chief was guarded by legions of eagle-eyed aides who let it be known, albeit obliquely, that the faintest mention of the subject would bring instant excommunication from the chain of command. To S Division's finest, who had long since learned to gauge the subtleties of the breezes that blew from headquarters, that was ominous enough.

There had been a time, of course, when the spectre of Robert Bishop did not stalk the corridors of power wreaking awful mental havoc. In that other time Robert Bishop had been just another name on the duty scheme ready to be sacrificed to the lofty cause of a soccer punch-up, political demonstration or plain old humdrum uniform patrol. When even the most sensitive analyst of political power would have cast an eye over the personnel file of Bishop R., without even raising an eyebrow. It was an uninspiring career by any standards. He had joined the job at 19 after a stint as an insurance clerk, had made inspector after 15 years which was pretty well par for the course, had spent the majority of his service with the patrol force apart from a couple of uneventful attachments to CID and the traffic division. Now in his late thirties his career seemed to have stalled altogether for he had been passed over twice for promotion. There was nothing remarkable about his physical appearance either; fair hair receding on top, a face that had never lost the uncertainty of adolescence, mild eyes behind the regulation plastic lenses of police issue spectacles. Yes, Bob Bishop had been a nonentity all right in those halcyon days before the great memo war changed everything and the MMP rose Phoenix-like from the ashes of battle.

The MMP was short for the Media Management Programme which had been devised by the PRO, a cerebral and mystical figure with a power source close to the Godhead. The PRO had been brought in by the new chief. He was a 42-year-old shooting star with newfangled ideas on how to run a police force, and it was rumoured that he had achieved his exalted position by deflecting the unwelcome attention of the news media when the chief's divorce attracted scurrilous stories of his predilection for cocktail barmaids. Another version had it that young and ambitious police wives had engineered their husband's advancement in rank by accommodating the energetic and youthful Chief Constable whilst on the routine rounds of police properties. In the event, no evidence emerged to support either hypothesis and the rumour-mongers retired in search of less well-defended targets. They all agreed that the PRO was 'a bloody fine flak eater'.

Not that anyone had any real inkling of the scale of the PRO's influence until the memo war was raging in earnest and casualties were falling like autumn leaves. The opening salvoes were fired from the chief's office and fell on the desks of his line commanders in the form of a photocopied discussion paper outlining 'MMP – the way ahead'. The accompanying memo bearing the chief's signature asked in the best democratic manner for observations on the principle of the proposals. Unaccustomed to this freedom of expression, stalwarts of the old guard waxed lyrical in their condemnation of the very idea. Before they could congratulate themselves on their newfound abilities to influence policy, they were either demoted or transferred. The next wave of memos called for practical suggestions to implement the programme. Dissenters once again found themselves suddenly out in the cold. And so the democratic process evolved until the memo war ended with wholehearted support for the chief's plan. The strategy was called man-management.

Having effectively out-manoeuvred the opposition, the next phase of the MMP called for the appointment of divisional media handlers (the more traditional title of press officer had been abandoned as lacking the definitive spirit of the enterprise). Working on the assumption that the average policeman can do anything provided the orders are bawled loudly enough, the personnel computer was quickly cranked up to produce ideal candidates for the job. The electronic impulses busied themselves within the data banks, logic elements picked the brains of the silicon chips, the machine hummed and purred contentedly as it juggled names and career profiles. Finally it punched up its recommendations on the hard copy printer. Beside the S Division code materialised the name – Bishop, Robert. Inspector. Uniform Patrol.

Quite what mysterious qualities the chosen few possessed over and above the 120 or so inspectors then serving, was not clear, but the computer had spoken and the chief constable had a touching faith in the ability of technology to winkle out talents lost to the mere mortal mind. Once the selection had been made not a moment was wasted, inspectors were pulled off their various assignments with indecent haste and whisked to the presence.

Bob Bishop emerged from his pep talk with the PRO, his mind reeling. He rushed home and confided in his wife: 'Janet love, I thought I was dreaming or something. There I was about to wear down a little more shoe leather on the old mean streets when they pulled me into headquarters and before I know it I'm sinking into the Wilton and sipping Bristol Cream and there's the PRO talking to me like I'm his long lost brother or something. If you'd asked me this morning I'd have said he wouldn't have known me from Adam. And there we were chatting like a couple of good 'uns. Me and the PRO! And you know what he said, just to sort of break the ice, he said don't go to Russia! That's what he said – don't ever go to Russia,

Bob, he said, because over there they think inspector is the highest police rank going and chief constables are 10 a penny. Then he told me he'd asked for me on his team and he'd got a green light from the chief. Boy you could've knocked me down with a feather. I'd've sworn he never even knew I existed.'

'You didn't tell me you were going to Russia,' his wife picked up the point, frowning.

'No – I'm not love,' Bishop said. 'That was just a figure of speech.'

'So what's this about Russia?'

'Nothing love – that's just the way he talks, you know? PROs know all that sort of thing.'

'Would they pay our moving expenses?'

'We're *not* going to Russia.'

'Good job anyway – it's too cold over there and I don't think I could get on with iron curtains.'

'Look love, *nobody's* going to Russia,' Bishop emphasised and he persuaded her to make him a cup of tea before announcing his new appointment as S Division's media handler.

'He didn't exactly tell me what I'd got to do,' Bishop said, 'but he gave me a good tip though. Told me to get myself a fancy waistcoat, one that'd knock your eye out. Nothing like a fancy waistcoat for projecting the image, he said. Throws 'em off balance. You've got to be up early in the morning to slip one past a fancy waistcoat. It's all psychological.'

'What sort of fancy waistcoat?' his wife asked dubiously.

A wide grin spread across Bishop's face. 'A red one,' he said thinking about the Russian anecdote which had cheered him enormously. 'A bright red one.'

Bishop had the waistcoats made up for him by a bespoke tailor who was getting on, but came recommended as an excellent craftsman. The request to make waistcoats brought tears of nostalgia to the old man's eyes and he made Bishop two of the vivid garments for the price of one on account of the pleasure the unusual order had given him.

The metamorphosis of Bob Bishop took place during a

IS IT A TRANSFER TO
THE K.G.B. DEAR ?
RAINBOW
POLICE
REVIEW

three-day course at headquarters during which the PRO prepared his fledgling media handlers for their new and challenging role. The moment they returned to the divisions they were met with frosty hostility.

On the S, Bob Bishop fared no better than the rest. Suspicion and resentment greeted him wherever he went. In the eyes of his colleagues he wasn't a copper any more, he was a traitor, a turncoat, an alien form. Not that the chilly reception worried him unduly for he was basking in the reflected power of the PRO who could transcend the rigidity of the chain of command and could bring severe retribution upon even the most mighty by merely picking up the telephone. Woe betide the senior officer who tried to pull rank on Bob Bishop.

Without seeming to lose face in front of their troops, the S Division hierarchy retired into a state of smouldering resentment. They vowed to bide their time, after all neither the chief nor his PRO would be around forever, and when the new day came, as it surely would, well sufficient to say they had good memories. In the meantime, Bob Bishop, waistcoat flashing imperiously under a sombre grey suit, strode purposefully down the corridors of power, wheeling and dealing and brushing aside mundane queries with his favourite expression: 'That's show-biz'. The transformation was complete.

When the *Close Up* team arrived to film an in-depth report on the Eastgate murder, Bob Bishop accepted the assignment with relish. Now that his eyes had been opened he quite fancied himself as a TV director and to work with one of the top TV current affairs shows further fired up his imagination. By the time the unit had finished a series of sequences in and around the police station to pin the subject down in time and place, Bob Bishop was well and truly in his element for the next phase demanded by the shooting script was a full blooded reconstruction of the crime itself.

They made their rendezvous according to Bob Bishop's meticulous instructions at the corner of Belvedere Road and Eastgate Drive, within a hundred yards of the spot where witnesses's accounts indicated that the girl had been snatched.

It was a cold gritty morning with dust blowing in the wind funnelled down into the canyons between the multi-storey blocks of flats which stretched as far as the eye could see. It was an asphalt and concrete wasteland interspaced with scrubby forlorn little trees from which the vandals had stripped bark and branches. Despite their bald state the trees had learned the Eastgate knack of survival. Here and there the drab vista was enlivened with lurid graffiti aerosoled on the concrete walls, vivid loops and whorls spelling out hideous obscenities. That was Eastgate.

Against this background the TV crew made an interesting study as they unloaded their gear from a convoy of Volvo estate cars. The cameraman and the second cameraman always worked together, like Siamese twins, humping tripod, spare magazines and assorted paraphernalia and then with loving care, the camera itself. They both wore blue jeans and fur-trimmed anoraks. They both had angular faces and blond hair. At a distance they looked about 16 years old. The sound recordist hefted a tape machine the size of a small suitcase and waggled his pistol microphone this way and that, checking sound levels. He had on an old grey woollen windcheater and with the headphones clamped over his brown curly hair was lost to the world as he twiddled knobs and checked gauges, his eyes reflecting a happy yet vacant expression. An electrician, who looked ready for anything in a camouflaged combat jacket, followed the other three around like a shadow, his jaws working mechanically on chewing gum. But the focal point of the crew was Dirk Lombard, the producer, an incredibly tatty wartime flying jacket draped casually over a plaid lumberjack shirt, his eyes moving incessantly as he worked out camera angles and reconciled the limitation of reality with the demands of his script. A continuity girl carried the schedule on a clipboard and kept the crew supplied with mint imperials and chocolate eclairs from a large handbag. Against these eager young faces the old man looked hopelessly incongruous, with his snowy white hair and spectacles dangling from a cord around his neck. He wore a shabby corduroy suit, heavy soled brogues and a floppy bow tie. He had to be pushing 70.

'See,' Dirk Lombard explained when Bishop asked the obvious question. 'On *Close Up* the writer's got control. We look over the scenario, write a tight script, work out a filming schedule then pull a crew together from freelances. That way we don't need a director poncing around buggering up a crisp story line.' He popped another mint imperial. 'See,' Lombard further explained the intricacies of his profession. 'The last thing we want is a director peeking down the camera and shooting sunsets and falling leaves, only the ACTT's got us by the balls. We got to have a five man crew minimum, sometimes six, if the electricians are bloody minded and squeal for a driver, otherwise the union's going to black us. Nobody moves a single muscle without a director, so we pick up some guy who won't cause us problems. See Donald over there, he's a nice old guy, all he's interested in is bee-keeping only he's got a director's ticket so he's pure gold.'

When an opportunity arose, Bishop tested this new insight into television practice.

'How's it going?' he asked the old man, during a break in filming.

'Too windy by half,' the old man replied.

'Oh – affects the camera, does it?'

'Plays up hell with the hives,' said the old man.

'See,' Dirk Lombard continued Bishop's tuition in the mysteries of the media. 'We got a good camera team there. Last crew out of Vietnam.' He pronounced it Veet-nam. 'No messing about with sunrise through trees or dew on blades of grass. Just in, get the job done and out in double quick time. Pure gold.' He reached into the girl's handbag and helped himself to a chocolate eclair.

By the time the *Close Up* team prepared to film the murder reconstruction, Bob Bishop was steeped in the trivia of television production. He stood on the street corner, his overcoat unbuttoned, thumbs hooked in the fob pockets of his waistcoat, squinting professionally over the scene. He had with him Jack Rivers, the detective superintendent from headquarters, who was wearing a silver grey Swedish coat and elevator heels which added a good two inches to his height.

From the moment he knew he was to appear on TV, Rivers had been endeavouring to achieve a Martini-ad effect in his style of dress which was spoiled by his nervous habit of fiddling with his flies, a little quirk of behaviour which had earned him the nickname Jack-the-Zipper.

Rivers scowled at the TV crew with growing apprenhension. 'What's going on?'

'Oh they're just going to shoot a little wallpaper, run a little wild track,' Bishop replied breezily.

Rivers blinked at the double talk. 'Sounds like a bloody freak show to me.'

'Relax Jack.'

'I told you – I don't want any mucking about. . . .'

'Take it easy,' Bishop told him soothingly. 'Everything's taken care of.'

'You said it'd only take a minute,' said Rivers accusingly, surreptitiously fiddling with his flies. 'We've been here hours already.'

'I was speaking figuratively Jack. Takes time to set up a sequence like this – that's show biz you know.'

'Bloody fiasco,' Rivers mumbled, beginning to get cold feet as the moment for him to go before the camera approached: 'I've got police work to do Bishop – you're going to have to get someone else.'

'Jack,' Bishop said. 'Trust me, will you. You're the investigating officer – this is your big moment. Think of the fan mail.'

'What fan mail?'

'Just a figure of speech, Jack, OK?'

Rivers fingered the zip of his trousers. 'I don't want any trick questions.'

'Jack don't worry – I'll take care of everything.'

'. . . or any clever stuff.'

'Relax.'

'What are you staring at?' Rivers clutched his throat. 'It's my tie isn't it?'

'What?'

'You don't like my tie, do you Bob?' Rivers cried. 'Oh

Christ, I knew I should've worn something else. You think my tie makes me look ridiculous – I know you do.'

'Your tie looks fine Jack – looks fine to me.'

'It's the suit then, I knew it – I should've worn the pin stripe.'

'Jack, relax will you? You look great, now just calm down while I get this show on the road.'

Rivers grabbed Bob Bishop's arm and asked desperately: 'And what's shooting wallpaper got to do with anything?'

Bishop disengaged himself and walked across to where the crew were setting up; idly wondering whether media handlers in other lines of work had to put up with prima donnas like Jack Rivers. He hadn't bulled up Rivers as the greatest detective since Sherlock Holmes to end up with his dancing a jig in the street all tongue-tied, camera-shy and fidgetting with his trousers. He went over to where Dirk Lombard was in conversation with the crew.

'Hey Dirk – I've got everybody champing at the bit – what's the hold up?'

The producer turned to him with a tortured expression: 'We're looking for something to establish the shot, you know, something evocative, something that tells the story.'

'You know,' said the first cameraman, 'when we were in Biafra we shot this great sequence to set up the story. . . .'

'Those guys kicking this kid,' said the second cameraman.

'We came in from the barren countryside,' confirmed the first cameraman, 'panned through the dust from a passing truck and then zoomed right in on 'em – beautiful shot.'

'Yellow filter all the way,' said the second cameraman.

'I see it!' Lombard exclaimed excitedly, 'the futility of life – solid gold!'

'What happened to the kid?' Bishop asked.

'What kid?' said the first cameraman.

'The kid they were kicking.'

They looked at him as though he was crazy.

Bishop cleared his throat and hooked his thumbs in his waistcoat. 'Look Dirk,' he said, 'I don't want to hurry you or anything, but I'd appreciate it if you could do the interview with Jack Rivers pretty soon, he's beginning to hop around a bit and I think he'll go off the boil if you leave him too long.'

With the haunted look still in his eyes, Dirk Lombard agreed to alter the schedule and sucked thoughtfully on a mint imperial as the continuity girl coaxed Jack Rivers into signing the disclaimer. The camera crew set up facing a gaunt block of flats on which was aerosoled the single word Anarchy, the A enclosed in a perfect circle.

When Rivers was in position, the sound man crouched down by his knees and thrust the sausage shaped microphone in the direction of Rivers' midriff. The second cameraman held a clapperboard in front of the detective's face and marked the shot. The first cameraman squinted into the eyepiece and said 'running' and they were away, swinging into their routine. Even the white haired director seemed vaguely interested in what was happening.

'Jack Rivers is one of this country's foremost criminal investigators,' said Dirk Lombard with oily familiarity. 'Yet the brutal slaying of this young girl may yet test his mettle as a crime buster. So tell me Jack, is this the most baffling case of your career to date?'

Rivers opened his mouth but no sound emerged, his fingers tightened around the zip of his trousers, his eyes rolled heavenwards as if seeking divine assistance. It wasn't the question they had rehearsed, but Rivers, his mind a blank could only stumble through his prepared answer.

'Oh yes – I remember it well,' he said in a strangled voice. 'I was home with the missus and we were just sitting down to tea when the 'phone rang to call me out. In a matter of minutes I was looking down at that poor child's body. . . .'

'Hold it!' The cameraman raised his eye from the viewfinder and gestured toward the block of flats. On the lower balcony a woman was putting out washing on a line. 'Washing coming out of his left ear,' said the cameraman, 'we'd better start again.'

By the time they had re-positioned, beads of sweat were standing out on Rivers' forehead. Bob Bishop thoughtfully

EASTGATE
COMMUNITY CENTRE
PIGS OU
EZZA
RULES
EASTGATE BOVER
GUTROT ALES & SPIRITS
EAT YOUR HEARTS OUT CROSSROADS

loaned him a handkerchief. The director wandered off to sit on a wall and stare into the distance.

'Running!' said the cameraman. The shot was marked.

'They call Jack Rivers, Britain's toughest detective,' purred Dirk Lombard. 'Yet the sight of a murdered child never fails to bring tears of compassion to his eyes. Tell me Jack, how many child slayings have you investigated?'

Rivers exhaled the breath he had been holding for an eternity, gasped for air and began to gabble as though his voice had been speeded up. 'Oh yes I remember it well. I was home with the missus and we were just sitting down to tea when the 'phone rang. . . .'

The cameraman raised his head again: 'Sorry Dirk,' he said, 'Hair in the gate. We'll have to do that one again.'

Bob Bishop couldn't bear to watch the third attempt at the interview. He went over to where the director was sitting staring at one of the tower blocks.

'Just like bees you know,' the old man said.

'What?'

'Just like a bloody great hive.'

'I never thought of it like that.'

'Oh yes – there's a lot more to bees than meets the eye. Did you ever see my documentary, *Sting of the French Black*?'

'Must've missed it,' Bishop apologised.

'Pity,' said the old man.

After a while Jack Rivers came bounding over, grinning hugely: 'Nothing to it Bob,' he said. 'Any time you want another interview, just give me a shout. I think I'll stick around and watch the rest.'

As they prepared to film the reconstruction itself, Dirk Lombard's expression grew more and more haunted. There was a minor hiccup when the electrician pointed out something they had all overlooked and that was the very real possibility that the film would be blacked because none of the participants were Equity members and an inter-union agreement was in force. After a discussion they agreed that although the sequence might technically be construed as acting, the clause on news film reconstruction was sufficient loophole for them to squeeze through if the point was ever challenged. With the problem resolved the continuity girl handed round chocolate eclairs.

Dirk Lombard took a walk by himself to get the theme clear in his mind. He was gone for a full 10 minutes during which time the crew hung about swapping yarns and then the director presented each of them with an autographed copy of a slim paperback he had written: *Beekeeping-made-easy*.

Bob Bishop found himself impressed by the lonely creativity of the TV business. When Lombard returned he looked even more agonised and called for mint imperials before bringing everyone together for an impromptu conference out of the wind in the cavernous foyer of one of the blocks of flats. Rubbing his hands together to generate enthusiasm Dirk Lombard said: 'Now we're going to shoot a nice tight movie, bags of actuality and gritty realism. I want to do this how-it-could-have-happened, rather than harden it up otherwise we'll get hassle from the legal eagles. So we're going to shoot from the roof of these flats with a long panoramic this-is-the-city scene setter to establish the shot, then we'll come down right into the street and there's the girl, she's walking down the street click-clack-click-clack, maybe five-six seconds of walking to build up the tension.'

'You'll want a wild track on that Dirk,' said the sound recordist.

'Bags of wild track – soak it up,' Lombard said. 'Then the car comes into the shot,' he continued, 'He's kerb crawling – crawl – crawl – crawl, two-three seconds maybe, get the viewers really wound up.'

'That's a long time to hold the shot Dirk,' said the cameraman, 'might help if we come out in between and pick up wallpaper.'

'We'll see how it goes,' said Lombard. He slapped a fist into his open palm. 'Then bang – we hit the action, the guy's out of the car and he grabs her, they struggle – let that run as long as we can – just out of focus, just fuzzy enough to give a sinister feel. Then he drags her into the car and away. Shot follows the car and then back to the empty street. Could be magic – solid gold.'

The sound man scratched his ear. 'We're going to need radio mikes, then?'

'Oh yeah – all the way.'

'We'll need the walkie-talkies for the cues,' chipped in the continuity girl, noting everything on her clipboard.

'Sure,' said Lombard, 'whatever works best.' He turned to Bob Bishop who was listening enthralled. 'How about your people Bob?'

Bishop said: 'Well the girl's a friend of the deceased, we've got her in identical clothing only her parents say they don't want her identified.'

'I'll talk to them,' said Lombard, 'put their minds at rest.'

'I've got the ugliest DC I could find to play the part of the villain and we've got a Cortina with the same number plates as the real car in case some clever bugger spots it.'

'That's magic Bob,' Lombard said, 'pure gold.' he looked around expectantly. 'Any questions?'

There were none.

'OK – let's do it.'

The girl was a typical Eastgate scrubber who thrust out her chest and wiggled her bottom provocatively when they explained her role in the reconstruction. Her parents' objection had been so effortlessly overcome that Bishop had a suspicion money must have changed hands. When everyone was in place he went up to the roof of the tower block with the crew and helped lug the equipment from the lift up two flights of concrete stairs. It was blowing like hell on the roof, the wind whistling through the aerials and wire contraptions strung around the flat deck. Dirk Lombard paced around peering over the parapet and then decided to set up in a corner which provided the best view of Eastgate Drive. The cameraman practised panning around while the second man worked the lens, and when he was happy with the arrangement he checked the counter on the camera and told Lombard: 'Not much left on this mag Dirk.'D'you want a change?'

'OK,' Lombard decided. 'Change the mag. I want to get this

in one good squirt.' While he was waiting he used his miniature Motorola to converse with the director and the police party in the street. The sound man was picking up the radio mikes at full strength. Only the electrician looked bored.

'Is everybody ready?' Lombard shouted simultaneously to the crew and into the radio once the new magazine was in place.

The second cameraman leaned out with his board: 'Running,' said the cameraman.

'Mark the shot,' said Lombard and into the radio: 'Cue the girl.'

The camera traverse began with a shot of the distant gas works and panned around through a hundred and eighty degrees winging over rooftops, sweeping the facades of the high rise towers, zeroing in on the street far below, going in tight on the girl walking down the pavement. Without raising his head from the eyepiece the cameraman said: 'The kid's waving Dirk.'

Lombard hurled himself at the parapet and peered anxiously downwards. In disbelief he saw the girl pause and wave cheerfully.

'For Chrissakes, keep the kid walking,' he shouted into the Motorola, and then to the camera crew: 'Keep it running!'

'The kid's running Dirk,' the cameraman informed him laconically, his eye still screwed to the view finder.

'Not the girl you fool!' Lombard yelled into the radio. 'Bloody kid,' Lombard muttered disgustedly to no one in particular. 'Should've used a midget.'

'It's OK Dirk,' the cameraman relayed the picture from his lens, 'she's walking again. . . . did you want her to swing her hips like that?'

Lombard groaned and then the continuity girl who was reading off the stopwatch said: 'Six seconds – Mark!'

'Cue the car,' Lombard yelled into the radio.

A squeal of tyres drifted up to them and Lombard leaped to the parapet again in time to see the mock-up Cortina burning rubber as it raced after the girl.

'What's that leadfoot think he's doing!' Lombard wailed.

'He's supposed to crawl – CRAWL!!'

'The girl's running now Dirk,' said the cameraman, 'here comes the car.' The sound man winced and raised his headphones: 'The kid's screaming blue murder Dirk.'

'Hey – this is good,' said the cameraman, 'terrific action, she's fighting with our guy now . . . yes . . . yes . . . he's dragging her into the car. Jesus! Will you look at that!'

They made the parapet in one bound. A beer truck had turned into the street below and several burly draymen, spotting a damsel in distress, had hurled themselves to the rescue. They were making mincemeat of the DC who was spreadeagled across the bonnet of the car. Before their eyes, Jack Rivers appeared sprinting down the street waving his arms, his expensive Swedish coat flapping about him as he tried to save his man from further punishment. One of the draymen, built like the truck he drove, turned and floored the detective superintendent with a right uppercut.

On the roof, Dirk Lombard turned to Bishop, his eyes shining with excitement. 'That's magic Bob – what a public co-operation story. A whole new angle – fresh – vital – what a movie – pure gold!'

Bob Bishop blinked and then smiled as Dirk Lombard capered around slapping him on the shoulder and whooping with delight. He hooked his thumbs in his scarlet waistcoat and grinned with pleasure as he carefully memorised all the technical details of this triumph in media handling. The continuity girl gave him a chocolate eclair.

Nine The Inspection

'OUGHT to pull those slums down,' observed Sir Ralph Hawk, eyeing the gaunt high rise blocks which stretched as far as the eye could see.

'No Sir Ralph,' Henry Grey attempted to explain, 'They already pulled the slums down. That's when they built those.'

'Look like slums to me,' the HMI persisted. 'Only one thing for slums – pull 'em down.'

'No you've got it wrong Sir Ralph,' Grey strove to elucidate his meaning. 'Slums were those nasty little back to back terraces patched up with corrugated iron. They pulled those down years ago.'

'Then what d'you call those monstrosities?' Sir Ralph waved a hand encompassing the great concrete wasteland.

Grey sought for the correct description. 'High rise dwelling units, er . . . vertical villages . . . oh what was that other one . . . ah yes, green concrete extrusion. You know Sir Ralph they built the top first then jacked it all up and built the rest underneath, floor by floor, for 22 storeys. . . .'

'Slums,' said the HMI succinctly. 'Whatever else you call them, they're still slums. Look at the side of that one, it's painted purple.'

'Ah, well you see, it began as natural concrete grey but the pollution made it so dirty they sprayed it purple – looks a lot better now.'

'Hideous,' said Sir Ralph. 'Look at that other one, with the girders – they're all rusty.'

This time Henry Grey was on surer ground. He liked to keep up to date with civil engineering techniques. 'That's not rust Sir Ralph. It's what the architects call patina. They intended it to look like that.'

'Don't be ridiculous Henry,' Sir Ralph Hawk told him bleakly. 'That's rust I tell you and these are all slums. Ought to be pulled down.'

'No, you don't understand,' The deputy chief tried again. 'They already pulled the slums down. . . .'

But it was no use. The HMI wasn't listening as he began to

stride purposefully away, head jerking, taking in the scene. Henry Grey had to hurry to catch up, his silver-topped cane tucked under his arm in the best military fashion. It had been a mistake, he'd known that from the start, but try as he might he couldn't deflect Sir Ralph Hawk from his desire to visit Eastgate, to see the scene of the crime for himself.

They'd been on their way to the incident room, a minor diversion from the inspection programme, to which Henry Grey had reluctantly agreed. The HMI called it showing the flag, a little morale booster for the troops. On the way, Sir Ralph had suddenly expressed a desire to see Eastgate, much to Grey's horror. They were behind schedule as it was. Even so, a brief spin around in the staff car wouldn't have been so bad, but when Sir Ralph had ordered the driver to stop and had leaped out of the limousine to set off on foot, Henry Grey had been beside himself and close to panic.

Even the most intrepid PC never ventured into Eastgate on foot. It was unheard of. Why in this neck of the woods even the Pandas patrolled in pairs in case of mechanical breakdown. Legend had it that a police car which broke down in this neighbourhood had been picked clean by the denizens of the concrete swamp before a breakdown truck could reach it; radio, wheels, battery and all removable parts already changing hands on the black market. It was not only unwise for a stranger to walk through Eastgate – it was plain suicidal. Or so Henry Grey had been lead to believe. Now he hurried after the HMI, eyes flitting this way and that, watchful for any surprise assault, hopeful that his apprehension was not too obvious. They couldn't have been more conspicuous, both in full uniform, fairly dripping silver braid.

When he caught up Sir Ralph Hawk said: 'Community involvement – just the ticket for slums like this Henry. Hearts and minds you know. You ought to get some community programme going down here.'

'But they hate us here Sir Ralph,' Grey replied, glancing fearfully at the knots of people gathering on street corners and the balconies of the flats to follow their progress through sullen eyes. 'It's hostile territory.'

I TOLD YOU SON, THESE COPPERS OF TODAY HAVE NO RESPECT AT ALL.
CRAPA
PIGS O
ACAB
NO GO AREA

'Nonsense man,' the HMI told him. 'All the more reason to get stuck in and show the flag.'

'Two PCs got lured out of their Pandas down here a couple of weeks ago,' Grey said glumly, 'both still in hospital.'

But the HMI wasn't listening. 'Hearts and minds Henry,' he expounded. 'Get something going with the young wives. Always a good place to start, young wives eh!' He winked at Grey. 'Then the kids, organise some play schemes, get some bingo going for the old folk. Blue Lamp Bingo, how's that for a winner Henry. You'd have 'em eating out of your hand in no time.'

Sir Ralph Hawk paused in mid-stride to amplify his point, jabbing a finger towards one of the more hideous blocks of flats rearing 20 storeys up into the gritty grey sky.

'You're right Henry – the vertical village,' he exclaimed with evangelical fervour as if some divine inspiration had suddenly struck him. 'That's the place to start – winning the old hearts and minds. Positive thinking, that's what I like to hear Henry – positive thinking.'

Suddenly from a balcony high above them something came flying down, something which splattered on the pavement close by and gave off an appalling stench. Henry Grey looked around desperately. He had given the staff car driver implicit instructions to shadow them closely, but now there was no sign of the limousine.

Splat! Something equally nasty hit a nearby wall. The smell was indescribable.

The deputy chief quickened his pace, fearful of what might happen next. Where the hell was that car!

'Puts me in mind of my old Padre,' Sir Ralph Hawk said, oblivious of any impending danger. 'Good fellow for stiffening up the line, putting a bit of backbone into 'em.'

Sock! Something narrowly missed Grey's head and as he instinctively glanced upwards, he could see that they were being pelted from the balconies with the evil contents of the long since blocked refuse shutes. Grey seized the HMI's arm and began to run.

'Jog do you Henry?' Sir Ralph said, trotting obediently as

Grey propelled him towards the comparative safety of the street corner. 'Good for the circulation, eh? Prefer a stiff brandy myself.'

The garbage gunners were beginning to find the range and the foul smell brought on a wave of nausea as Henry Grey bustled the HMI around the corner. As he paused to catch his breath the staff car miraculously appeared, tracking rubber as it raced to rescue them for the bombardment.

Henry Grey breathed a sigh of relief as he sank into the back seat while the driver gunned the limousine out of the danger zone.

Sir Ralph Hawk was unperturbed . 'That old padre,' he said, shaking his head at the memory, 'kept 'em on their toes all right Henry. Ought to take a leaf our of his book. Hearts and minds and Wog.'

The deputy chief wondered if he had heard correctly. 'Did you say Wog Sir Ralph?' he inquired as casually as he could.

'Wrath of God,' replied the HMI with a twinkle in his eye.

Ten The First Police Astronaut

BRILLIANT. Philip Lawson was quite brilliant. Two university degrees, effortlessly obtained, law on the one hand, economics on the other, a razor sharp mind; a photographic memory. And that wasn't all, not by a long chalk. Apart from his academic brilliance, Philip Lawson was a fitness fanatic with a natural ability to do everything well. He could out-run, out-swim, out-squash, out-tennis, in fact he could outplay just about everybody in sight. He was strikingly handsome with dark hair, an engaging smile and a slight downturn of the mouth which added an extra degree of interest to his face. With this abundance of talent just why he'd joined the police force was a source of constant amazement to his superiors and a topic of endless envious argument among those he left behind on his meteoric rise through the ranks. By the time he was 36 he was an assistant chief constable, but then, in the two years that followed while he waited in the wings for a deputy's chair to fall vacant, a strange thing happened. Philip Lawson grew bored with success.

Like so many clever men whose chosen work no longer stretched their abilities, he began to construct a shell of eccentricity around himself which could be manipulated at will. He gave up looking for the next logical move in his career and started to amuse himself. To the horror of the staid, conservative, super-traditional hierarchy, Philip Lawson took to driving a battered '42 Willys, had his hair butchered into a severe crew cut and began talking in the jargon of the late sixties manned space flight programme.

The overall effect was so unnerving that the rest of the brass immediately shied away from 'that lunatic Lawson', fearful that whatever had afflicted him might just be contagious and so affect their own prospects of advancement. In short order he became the pariah of the top corridor, a dangerous extrovert abandoned to his own devices as brother officers paled visibly whenever he approached, retreating behind the locked doors of their offices. And Lawson, who had played their game so assiduously over the years, felt as though a great weight had been lifted from his shoulders. He had fired his main booster and was coasting free of the gravitational pull of the police force.

* * *

Philip Lawson woke instantly. The amazing transistorised man, no power surge needed, no warm-up necessary. When sleep was concluded the shift to full consciousness was accomplished within the blink of an eye. With the flat of his hand he massaged his stubbly scalp then reached out to the bedside table and picked up his wristwatch. The Omega Speedmaster hung from his fingers. NASA approved. First timepiece on the moon. Pleasantly heavy. In the pre-dawn darkness Philip Lawson held the watch close to his face and consulted the complicated luminous dial. It was 6 am. Earth time.

He slipped out of bed taking care not to disturb his wife. Mornings were better when he didn't disturb Lois. They had been married six years. Six years of good old dependable marriage during which her ambition had run in harness with his. Safe, predictable, successful, bountiful years. And what an attractive couple they made, so perfect for each other. Such a social asset, the lovely Lois. Now she didn't understand him. She didn't understand whey he wanted to wander around the house wearing a tee shirt and a baseball cap. She didn't understand why he wanted to trade in the Alfa with its tinted windows and eight-track stereo for a beaten-up Army jeep, nor his obsession with manned space flight. She even thought Neil Armstrong was some influential civil servant in the Home Office. No, better not to disturb Lois, with that hurt look spoiling her pretty face. She didn't understand anything any more.

Philip Lawson crept downstairs, his bare feet padding silently on the soft pile of wall to wall Wilton. It was a vast modern house with an abundance of pastel shaded bathrooms-en-suite, the accommodation planned for leisure-living, tastefully furnished by Lois from the very best repro-collections.

Air conditioning hummed softly in the background. He went to the basement room which he had fitted out as a small gymnasium. Here the scene was very different. The room was spartan in its simplicity with wall bars and an assortment of equipment designed to keep the body in shape.

This morning Lawson selected the exercise cycle. He set the friction control, gripped the handlebars and began to push the pedals. A seven mile bike ride before breakfast without leaving the comfort of your own home. He worked up a good healthy sweat, felt the muscles and sinews of legs and stomach responding to the treatment, closed his eyes and imagined himself speeding down country lanes. He opened them again to stare stoicly at the blank white walls as the gauge racked up artificial miles. Nothing like a good bike ride to work out all those niggling frustrations and set you up for the day. See, you can even control the terrain with the little lever of the handlebars; up hill, down dale, swooping along until the sweat flowed freely.

After half an hour he dismounted and took a shower, stinging needles of hot then cold toning up his skin until his body glowed with pink health. Wrapped in his rough cotton robe, rubbing his hair with a towel, Lawson went up to the kitchen and made himself a small pot of Earl Grey. He put on his baseball cap with the NASA emblem, sat at the leisure-living breakfast bar and drank two large cups of the fragrant tea with the same deliberation he had taken his exercise. It was standard astronaut training to replace liquid loss as quickly as possible and a good astronaut needed to be both fit and purposeful. As he sipped his tea he heard the voice of NASA reaching out to him through deep space:

'Ranger-One – this is Houston Cap-com – good morning. Can you give us an update at this time?'

'Copy Houston,' Lawson said to himself. 'We're riding straight down the go-plot. Everything here is AOK.'

'Ranger, we copy that. OK Phil at the mark you are go for trans-lunar insertion.'

'Copy.' Lawson repeated. 'Let's make that a good burn Houston – on the button.'

Lawson smiled into his tea cup. A good astronaut needed a keen sense of mission. And the mission to-day was S Division promotion board. He had planned the occasion as the ultimate in police space flight. It was to be an outstanding achievement for mankind.

After a light breakfast, he returned to the master bedroom. Lois was still asleep. He left her a cup of tea, kissed her lightly on the forehead and then dressed in his best uniform, taking pains to ensure that everything was just so. When he was satisfied with his appearance, he went down to the garage where much to his wife's disgust he kept the wartime Willys. With its drab khaki paintwork and knobbly tyres the old Army jeep was the anachronism of modern motoring.

The metal seats were thinly padded and the design purely functional with no concession to comfort. In four wheel drive the jeep guzzled petrol and rode flat out at 60 mph. But that was the best 60 Lawson had ever ridden, sitting upright behind the square windscreen, the wind whistling around his ears. He loved that jeep with all his heart. He couldn't help the affectionate grin which spread across his face as he swung into the driver's seat and reached for the old-fashioned toggle starter. He was hearing the voice of NASA.

'Banger-One – we have ignition sequence.'

'Copy.'

'You are go for staging.'

'On board systems are go.'

'Ignition minus three – two – one – '

Lawson gunned the motor and roared out of the garage to the euphoria of mission control.

'That's a good burn, Phil, the bird is go.'

Foot hard down he raced through the stockbroker belt on course for the S. Division headquarters.

* * *

Unlike the line commanders, assistant chief constables were the executive wing of police management, the trusty right arm of the chief himself. They busied themselves with the executive function of translating policy into practice, wrestling with thorny management problems, issuing orders and directives down the chain of command, stamping hard on any lesser rank who gets too big for his boots.

The ACCs wielded the power of the chief himself and lorded it over their immediate subordinates, the chief superintendents, who ran divisions or departments. In turn, the chief superintendents who were subjected to this straighten-up-and-fly-right doctrine, lorded it over their subordinates, the superintendents, chief inspectors, inspectors and sergeants, right down the line to the troops to whom they never ever spoke unless absolutely necessary. Everyone lorded it over the PCs who in their turn wielded massive power mainly through the canteen mafia, by virtue of strength of numbers. The chief would pale visibly whenever a PC was mentioned and thus the subtle balance of power within the police force was maintained on an even keel.

When Philip Lawson became the first police astronaut he threw the system out of kilter and for a while chief superintendents would be seen in animated conversion with PCs and chief inspectors found the strain intolerable. None of this, of course, affected the one unassailable bastion of police democracy – the promotion board. Promotion boards were unstoppable, through flood and tempest, fire and famine. The bureaucratic machine rolled on and on and on, for promotion boards were based on the democratic principle that every man must have his chance. The logic was simple. Any self-opinionated officer who woke up one day with the half-baked notion that he deserved promotion could fill in the appropriate form and was guaranteed a hearing before a promotion board constituted of one officer of assistant chief constable rank or above, his divisional commander, and a third member of superintendent rank. Once the notion of promotion boards caught on there was no stopping them. Promotion boards sat day in, day out, ad infinitum. A fine tribute to fair, impartial, democratic police management, a major advance on the old style where promotions were made in heaven rather than by

GROUND CONTROL HERE COMES MAJOR TOM
FLORIDA
DISNEYWORLD
SEA WORLD
FLY DIRECT WITH
GROTTYGLOBE
USA
US

dint of personal effort. But above all promotion boards were a royal pain in the neck.

By the time he arrived at S Division headquarters, Assistant Chief Constable Philip Lawson had achieved escape trajectory and had shut down on-board systems for the trans-lunar coast. He had plenty of time to spare before preparing for the next burn which would place him in moon orbit. He parked the Willys in the white lined parking space reserved for the Chief and strode jauntily into the building. Maxwell Cheep was waiting for him.

The divisional commander saluted stiffly: 'Morning sir – nice morning sir – did you have a good drive over sir?'

'Cheep, you look awful,' Lawson said.

In truth Maxwell Cheep did look pretty ghastly. His ashen face betrayed a haunted expression and his dark sunken eyes flickered nervously as he spoke.

'Oh no sir – just a touch of the old gastric upset.' His voice had a hollow ring as though the man had shrunk inside the shell of his body and was calling out from some internal cavern.

'Bert Holder sitting with us to-day?' Lawson asked, removing his brown leather gloves and slapping them against the palm of his hand.

The divisional commander's expression became even more pained: 'He didn't show up sir. He never does. If you ask me. . . .'

But the protest was lost on Lawson who mentally dismissed Cheep from further consideration. The man had failed his pre-flight. No sense of mission.

They went up to the oak panelled conference room where the promotion board was convened. The substitute third man turned out to be an eager superintendent from the training school who was so anxious to make a good impression that he said nothing least he should be misinterpreted and confined himself to vigorous nodding. Today's boards were constable to sergeant.

The first candidate was a beefy PC with curly hair and blunt

Slavic features who sat before them hunched forward, hands hanging awkwardly between his knees.

'Name?' Lawson asked briskly.

'Danvers, sir.'

'Want to be a sergeant Danvers?'

'Yes sir.'

'Qualified three years.'

'Yes sir.'

'What's your job?'

'Collator sir.'

Actually Lawson had all this information on the file in front of him, but the preliminary questions were designed to put the candidate at ease. They covered nice safe neutral ground.

'Length of service?'

'Eight years, sir.'

'Wife and two kids.'

'Right.'

'Owner occupier.'

'Four years now, sir.'

'Tell me about police work Danvers.'

The man blinked as the questioning shifted from the safe ground directly into a quicksand.

'Sir?'

'Tell me about being a collator then – what's it like?'

'What's it like, sir?'

'That's it – that's the question.'

'It's like being a collator, sir.'

'OK – what is a collator's function?'

'A collator's function, sir?' Danvers' brow creased into worried furrows. The going was getting tough.

'Yes – the question is – what is a collator's function?'

'To collate, sir.'

Lawson smiled. 'Very good,' he said, 'now we're getting somewhere. Tell me Danvers, exactly what is it that a collator collates.'

The furrows deepened: 'What is it a collator collates, sir?' Watch your step now, Danvers told himself, this is one of those trick questions the Federation reps warned you about.

'Precisely,' Lawson said.

'Well sir – this and that I suppose, sir – on cards, sir.'

'What would this and that be exactly, Danvers.'

'Hard to say, sir – we get so much of it. All sorts of stuff. We type it up on cards and enter it in the index.'

'What sort of stuff Danvers?'

'Well, sir – just this and that I'd say.'

'And what happens to all this "stuff" after you've typed it and entered it into the index?'

'It stays there, sir,' Danvers answered brightly.

'And what happens then?'

Danvers' eyes widened in surprise. ACCs certainly asked silly questions. 'Why nothing, sir – it's just part of the system.'

Lawson handed over the questioning to Maxwell Cheep. In the green glow of the command module he ran through a routine check-list and as he read off the instruments he could see that something was wrong.

'Houston this is Ranger-one. Read me?'

'Copy Ranger – read you on the high gain.'

'Houston I have a problem here – power down on the guidance system. Pings are blind.'

'Copy Ranger, will run that down, stand by.'

'Roger.'

'We see your problem now, Phil.'

'Copy Houston – what's my status?'

'Negative – negative Ranger-One. You are in an abort mode. I say again, the mission is in abort mode.'

'Copy that Houston — I'll work on it. Keep you advised.'

'Ranger-one, this is Houston Cap-com, good luck Phil.'

The next candidate was an aggressive young man with a toothbrush moustache who thrust out his jaw and tried not to stare at Lawson's astronaut crew cut.

'Ashton?' Lawson read from the file.

'Yes, sir.'

'Twenty-three eh?'

'Yes, sir.'

'Four years in the job?'

'Cadet before that, sir.'

MEGA BOOSTER
U.S.A.
APPO
IF YOU DON'T MIND ME SAYING SO, YOU LOOK A SHADE SPACED OUT SIR

'I see here you qualified for sergeant straight out of probation.'

'Yes sir – first opportunity I had.'

'Eager for promotion Ashton?'

'I think I'm ready for it sir.'

'Razor sharp I'll bet.'

'I like to think so sir.'

Lawson leaned back: 'Tell me about yourself.'

'Sir I'm an all-round professional police officer – two attachments with CID, a year and a half with the traffic division and now the Special Patrol Group, working all the while to broaden my experience.'

'What I meant,' Lawson said, 'was, tell me about yourself. What d'you do when you get off duty?'

'Study for my inspectors sir – the correspondence course.'

'Don't you ever think about anything else apart from the job?'

'No, sir – don't have the time.'

'Do you like the SPG?'

'Oh yes, sir – it's the real job. We really hammer 'em – it's the only language they understand.'

'And that's police work?'

'Right, sir.'

'D'you know what the S.4B is?'

Ashton hardly paused: 'Section of the Vagrancy Act of 1842 sir – we use that one all the time when we're hammering 'em.'

Lawson let Cheep take up the questioning while he responded to mission control.

'Ranger, this is Houston Cap-com. We've got your problem on the simulator Phil.'

'Copy.'

'Rockwell have it on the S.4B mock-up and we're running through the sequence from launch. We're working on it.'

'Roger Houston, copy that. The Saturn's a good bird.'

He had fair hair, the third candidate, fair hair razored into a severe crew cut, even features and an amiable expression. He smiled easily.

'Name?'

'Ross, sir.'

'What are your duties, Ross?'

'UBP car sir,' he said, using the correct definition of the Panda car.

'Qualified sergeant and inspector?'

'Yes, sir.'

'And what's your opinion of police work, Ross.'

'Sir I'm a student of the doctrine of maximum illusion.'

Lawson was surprised as he felt the first gentle tug of intellectual stimulus. 'Can you define that?'

'Oh yes, sir, I'd be happy to. Shall I start with the subjective or objective analysis?'

'Let's start subjective and see how we go.'

'Well sir – I'm the working cog in the unit beat machine. Because the rest of the machine is rusted up or simply not functioning, or incomplete, the cog which is me has to sustain perpetual motion, creating an illusion that the machine is really humming.'

'Clarify that for me, Ross.'

'Sir, I'm the illusion on the street. I, that is, the system, must keep moving 24 hours a day otherwise the machine will grind to a halt. I just drive the car around and around, I dare not stop. When my shift's over I hand it on to the next man. A perpetual illusion.'

'You don't talk to people?'

Ross shook his head: 'There's no need,' he said, 'there's nobody on the streets any more, they're all at home watching television.'

Lawson pursed his lips: 'Where did your doctrine of maximum illusion originate?'

'Ah you mean the objective view sir. I took my understanding of the police system and held it up to a mirror and there was no reflection. That's when I knew it was an illusion.'

'You mean you felt that our best endeavours to graft technology onto a creaking 19th century police structure had just evaporated?'

Ross nodded. His face was serious but behind the expression he was still smiling. 'The powers-that-be foisted the unit beat scheme onto a gullible service as a cure-all remedy. The service foisted the same illusion onto the public. It was the perfect vanishing act.'

'You know that's treason Ross?'

'Oh yes, sir.'

'And it doesn't worry you?'

'Not a bit. That's the beauty of the doctrine of maximum illusion. The more you study it the less tangible it becomes, and you yourself, being a part of it, become the greatest illusion of all. How can a shadow of something that doesn't exist contemplate treason. It's impossible.'

'So what is your ambition, Ross?' Lawson asked, his curiosity aroused. 'For instance, why did you ask for this board?'

'To perpetuate the illusion,' Ross replied earnestly. 'To widen the vision. The more you progress the better the possibilities, the greater the scope.'

'Your doctrine isn't complete then?'

'By no means,' Ross said emphatically. 'As a sergeant the illusion changes to a new perspective. My ambition is to develop new frontiers.'

'But what do you think about, Ross, in this state of perpetual illusion. What keeps you going?'

'It gives you time sir,' Ross replied. 'Time to consider new concepts. I have been a Russian chess master, a concert pianist, and Arctic explorer. Its not hard once you get started. you see I police the far reaches of the mind, the distant orbits of the imagination.'

'How about manned space flight?'

Ross shook his head sadly and a faraway look came into his eyes. 'Sir, I have flown with Saint-Exupery over the deserts – how does it go? Oh yes – with life flowing through you like a river, and the body in its dizzying flight, launched on it like a dug out canoe.' He smiled slightly as he recalled the quotation. 'But space flight – ah – too advanced for me at the moment. I'm only just getting started, feeling the way. I had hoped to be the first policeman in space, but I'm afraid others will get there before me. One man can only do so much.'

Lawson nodded as he handed the questioning over to Maxwell Cheep. All at once the mission was imperative.

'Houston, this is Ranger-One.'

'Copy Ranger.'

'Power looks stable now. Pings looking good. Request mid-course correction for lunar orbit insertion.'

'Roger. This is Cap-com Houston. Your decision Phil, burn or abort.'

'Houston I'm go for the burn.'

'Roger – three minutes to burn Ranger.'

Lawson relaxed. For a moment there, it has been touch or go, but he had willed the spacecraft to heal itself. Willpower and a sense of mission. But he had to hurry. There were other younger men coming up fast, men like Ross, eager to achieve the impossible. There was no time to waste.

When the promotion boards ended Maxwell Cheep button-holed him and adopting the obsequious manner he habitually reserved for senior officers, said:

'Sir you know we've got this murder inquiry over at Eastgate. Just a run of the mill case really, nothing to worry about of course, my men are pretty well on top of the situation, only . . . well sir, as you're visiting the division I wondered whether you had any advice for us . . . bearing in mind your vast experience in this kind of investigation. I mean, where should we be looking.'

'You must look everywhere,' Lawson replied firmly.

'But what should we be looking for sir?'

'You must look for everything,' Lawson told him, lending the full weight of authority to his words.

Privately he had no interest in Maxwell Cheep with his haunted expression and constant visits to the bathroom, with his oily manner and preoccupation with trivia. He needed to muster every ounce of concentration for the next phase of the mission. The powered descent to the surface of the moon.

Eleven The Inspection

MOST days during the inspection there was a little time set aside when Henry Grey found himself left to his own devices. Blanks had been left in the schedule at the express request of Sir Ralph Hawk who would disappear for an hour or so, presumably to meditate, doze, or simply reflect upon the onerous duties of Her Majesty's Inspector of Constabulary. Whenever this happened, Henry Grey, a stickler for punctuality, would more often than not pace fretfully, worrying about the possible disruption of his impeccable timetable. But on this particular day when the HMI repaired to a private room immediately after lunch, Grey borrowed an office in the S Division headquarters, took a memorandum pad from his briefcase and set it on the desk in front of him.

Now that he was alone his anger began to manifest itself. It was intolerable. After that discraceful scene in Eastgate they had paid an impromptu visit to the incident room and it had been a fiasco from start to finish. Quite intolerable. Toothbrush moustache bristling, Henry Grey took out his fountain pen and in his usual fastidious manner examined the memo pad for any blemishes before he began to write. In a neat spiky hand he addressed the memo to one of his immediate subordinates, the assistant chief constable responsible for CID supervision.

'I trust I do not need to remind you,' he began to write, 'that as the discipline authority of this police force, I do not suffer fools gladly, neither do I expect to be treated to a pathetically transparent attempt to pull the wool over my eyes by buffoons masquerading as detectives.' Committed to paper, Grey's words appeared more pompous than ever. 'Today,' he continued to write, 'I had the misfortune to escort Sir Ralph Hawk, the HMI, to the major incident room S Division, staffed by personnel under your command. The performance of these officers, upon our unheralded arrival, was below standard and unacceptable.' He underlined the last four words. 'It seems to me inconceivable that detectives could be engaged upon legitimate inquiries in billiard halls and public houses which appeared to be the case. Work in the incident room itself was sloppy undisciplined and certain female members of the staff were out of uniform in so much as they were wearing jeans, tight jeans,' again he underlined the words, 'which left little to the imagination.' Grey paused for a moment, pen hovering above the pad, 'Your detectives were scruffy in appearance, wearing leather jackets and polo-neck pullovers and others had removed their ties. One of the telephone lines appeared to have been reserved for the express purpose of placing horse racing bets.' The neat lines of the long hand paraded across the memo pad with military precision. 'Upon our arrival, a scene which I can best describe as chaotic, ensued and there was much shouting and waving of arms. The detective superintendent in charge appeared incapable of coherent conversation and constantly fiddled with the zipper of his trousers. Fortunately the HMI seemed impervious to these shortcomings although he did show inordinate interest in the women officers previously mentioned.' Grey reflected on the memory, pen poised, and then continued to write: 'I am of course aware that when CID officers are engaged on protracted and arduous inquiries, procedures may well be relaxed in the prevailing circumstances. However, I would be failing in my duty if I was to condone, or appear to condone, the obviously irregular behaviour of your incident room personnel. I must remind you that we are a disciplined force.' He underlined disciplined with two pen strokes, 'and that it has not escaped my notice that certain elements within the CID seemed to have adopted a most cavalier attitude towards their duties and personal appearance. Their unswerving allegiance to some mythical notion of police duty is quite unacceptable. Today's events only serve to confirm my opinion that CID officers are not to be trusted with the investigation of crime. It is therefore my duty to instruct you to reprimand these officers, however unpalatable, it may seem, because . . . .'

Here Grey stopped writing and a frown creased his brow. It had suddenly occurred to him that the ACC to whom he was addressing such vitriolic remarks had been a detective for much of his service and was bound to take the rebuke personally.

He gritted his teeth as he forced the pen down to the paper again. Never let it be said that Henry Grey shirked his duty on account of personalities.

He tried to continue writing but his hand was paralysed and refused to respond. Another more important consideration had flashed a warning signal in his mind. The ACC, he now recollected, also held the unofficial franchise for car tyres at quite remarkable discount.

Grey stared at the memo as he wrestled with his conscience. These were the horns of a dilemma and his frown deepened as he contemplated the consequences.

He sat immobile for several moments tapping his fountain pen against his teeth in consternation. No – he decided reluctantly, tearing the memo from the pad and carefully shredding it into the wastepaper basket. He couldn't afford to antagonise such a man. The treads on his Rover were wearing thin.

Twelve Psychic Squad

BERT ROYAL was chewing Neutradonna. When he spoke his lips were flecked with particles of the white stomach tablet.

'Oh come on, guvnor,' Royal appealed plaintively. 'You've got to be joking!'

'Bert,' Brian Webber replied, leaning back in his chair and flexing the cramps out of his shoulders: 'I'm doing you a favour – look at it that way. A nice cushy number.'

'Listen,' Royal pleaded. 'Couldn't you swing it on one of the sergeants. Any one of 'em knows the form.' He was paunchy, balding and tired looking. As he spoke his fleshy nose with its latticework of broken capillaries wrinkled to signify his displeasure. 'How about Jones, he's a good 'un. He could handle it easy.'

'Bert,' Webber said, fascinated by the white flecks on Royal's lips. 'I can't spare a man, you know that. The guvnor'd have my hide. So just humour me, OK?'

'Or Arthur Jenkins – Arthur knows the job inside out.'

'Arthur the statement reader,' Webber said patiently. 'I've got to keep continuity here, you know that.'

'Well Christ, there's got to be somebody.'

'Yes,' Webber said in a flat tone which brooked no further argument. 'You Bert. You're just the man for the job. You've got a nice line in chat.'

'Bullshit!' Royal moaned.

'Call it what you like,' Webber smiled, lacing his fingers behind his head and exercising his neck muscles. It felt good. He had been at the paperwork for six hours straight and things were beginning to seize up. He needed to unwind. 'Look Bert,' he said, 'Don't take it so personally. If there was an alternative I'd do it, you know that. Only . . . . well you know the score, we're stretched right out on this job. The squad's no help while they've got this Zatopec thing around their necks, so I'm just going to have to pull rank this once and you're going to have to knuckle under. But don't think I like it any more than you do.'

'I could sit in for Jenkins. . . .'

'No dice. I'm telling you Bert, this one's down to you so you might as well get used to it. Look on it as a bit of a challenge.'

'Thanks a lot.'

'No – I mean it. You might learn something.'

'Guvnor, I'm no good at this poncy stuff.'

'Put it down to experience Bert – what's that you're chewing anyway? Looks like chalk.'

'Stomach powder,' Royal replied miserably. 'Either I keep this stuff going down or the gut-burn gets me. What a choice.'

'Well see if you can make a good impression, eh Bert. OK it's a screwy idea, but you never know your luck.'

'Mine blew out years ago,' Royal said.

'Well look – put on your best suit, wipe that tragic expression off your face and just wheel 'em around, OK? What's so hard about that?'

'I don't like it.'

'Nobody likes it,' Webber returned to his paperwork, 'But we're stuck with it. Think what you can tell your grandchildren – the day I lead the psychic squad!'

Royal breathed a long sigh. 'Sure you won't change your mind?'

Webber didn't look up.

When Detective Inspector Bert Royal came out of Webber's office the old duodenal was playing up again, punching holes through his abdomen like a red hot poker. Worse than ever. Stabs of pain alternating with longer bouts of nagging ache. Unpredictable, creeping up unawares. Whenever he got excited or upset he could count on the ulcer to cut him in two. He went down the corridor slowly, wrestling with the pain which just lately had begun to frighten him badly. The doctor had told him if it got any worse there's be no alternative but the operation. The prospect scared him even more than the pain. It was a vicious circle. Light duties, the force surgeon had ordered, no stress, no shifts, special meals, plenty of rest. That or the knife. Ever since then Bert Royal had been swallowing Neutradonna and trying to disguise the pain. But he couldn't fool himself much longer. It was getting worse.

Once, before he had become preoccupied with his stomach,

Royal had been a damned fine detective with a hatful of commendations for excellent CID work. Five years ago when he'd joined the S Division on promotion to DI, he'd burned the midnight oil, set the pace in the pub with double Bells, worked round the clock for days at a stretch, carving out a reputation for nicking quality villains. Then one day, without warning, something had given under the strain, snapping like an elastic band. For the past two years he'd been a passenger just coasting along, nursing his ulcer and worrying himself sick as his hair receded and his complexion took on an unhealthy pallor. Now, as he looked at his watch, he sourly confessed to himself that he was hitting rock bottom, sweeping up the dog ends of a murder inquiry he would have eaten for breakfast in the old days. And to cap it all, there was Brian Webber telling him to nursemaid a bunch of nutters and weirdies. The psychic squad! Jesus, was this what he'd finally come down to? Time was when he'd have spit in Webber's eye at the mere suggestion. He wandered aimlessly down through the police station and ended up in the courtyard where his car was parked, slipped behind the wheel and started the engine. The thing he needed most was moral support, a friend to confide in.

Up on the CID floor, Detective Superintendent Jack Rivers poked his head around the door of Webber's office.

'I'm down in the incident room then, Brian.'

'Right you are, guvnor.'

'Everything OK?'

'Coming along.'

'How about the psychic squad?'

'No problem. All fixed up. Bert Royal's taking care of it.'

'Bert, eh?'

'He'll be all right.'

'Oh sure, I was just asking that's all.'

'He'll take care of it.'

'Does Royal know the form?'

'Briefed him myself.'

'That's all right then.'

'Uh-huh.'

By the expression on his face Rivers seemed about to confide in Webber. Instead he fiddled with the zip of his trousers and pulled a face '. . . well, anyway, God preserve us from nutters, eh Brian.'

'Right, guvnor,' Webber agreed. 'Amen to that.'

* * *

Bert Royal parked his 10-year-old Vauxhall in a police slot outside the mortuary block at the County General Hospital and went inside. He walked down to the police office and found Tony Mallow the assistant coroner's officer, inside, chair tipped back, feet on the desk, playing a harmonica softly and scribbling in a notebook resting on his knee.

Mallow was a PC who worked in plain clothes although that definition was questionable for today he was wearing an orange shirt with a yellow polka dot tie. Mallow had just one ambition in life and that was to write the winning tune in the Eurovision Song Contest. He concentrated on this ambition to the exclusion of everything else.

'Hi, Cap,' he called out running the harmonica across his mouth as Royal came through the door. The DI scowled. Mallow also had an unfuriating habit of ignoring the niceties of rank and addressing everybody in mid-Atlantic slang.

'Listen to this. . . .' He trilled an opening on the mouth organ and began to sing. 'Roop – boop- roo – boo – bee – doo.'

Royal sniffed. 'Mallow,' he said stiffly. 'Where's the inspector?'

'Oh back there,' The PC replied, nodding towards the mortuary beyond the glass partition. 'They're cutting one up.' Royal turned to leave but Mallow called him back. 'Hey Cap, you haven't heard the best bit. How about this for a lyric – Roop – boop – roo – boo – bee – doo – don't run with the herd; don't hunt with the pack – I'm the lone wolf – roop – boop – roo – boo – bee – doo. . . . .'

'I'm going through,' Royal said, but Mallow called him back again.

WHERE'S THE INSPECTOR? NO I DON'T KNOW THAT ONE, MUST BE AN OLDIE.
THE HIP BONE IS CONECTED TO THE LEG BONE
THE LEG BONE TO THE KNEE BONE
THE KNEE BONE TO THE OTHER BIT
DYLAN
MELODY MAKER

'Better sign the book, Cap – the coroner's a stickler for detail.'

As Royal wrote his name in the log, Mallow treated him to another toot on the harmonica.

'See, Cap,' he said, 'get an original A-side then on the flip re-soup a golden oldie – see how this grabs you . . . like a rubber ball, baby that's all that I am to you – bouncy – bouncy – bouncy, see solid rock, give it a twist, but of funky rhythm – what d'you say Cap – a winner?'

But Bert Royal was already out of the office walking through into the mortuary. He found his friend Stan Ogwill who ran the coroner's office, sitting on a stool eating a doughnut and drinking a cup of coffee.

A pathologist, his gown blood spattered, was working on a body laid out on the slab, meticulously recounting his progress on a miniature tape recorder dangling around his neck. With a jaundiced eye Ogwill watched him work.

'Hello Bert,' he greeted Royal, without surprise. 'What's this – business or social?'

Royal shrugged. 'I was just passing, Stan. How's tricks?'

'Pretty fair.'

Royal looked across at the post mortem. 'What's the job?'

'DOA,' Ogwill said, biting into his doughnut. 'Drugs OD if ever I saw one.'

'I just bumped into Mallow,' Royal said. 'He's mad as a nit, Stan, d'you know that?'

Ogwill drained the paper cup. 'He keeps sending his songs to the chief, anonymously of course. Somebody said they heard him humming one in the office. Come on through.'

Royal went with him to his room and Ogwill said: 'Don't talk to me about PCs, Bert, I had a couple keel over this morning on a training visit and another took a nose dive in the chapel of rest. No stomach for it any more.'

Ogwill was an old timer with 30 years in the job, a broad backside and infinite patience. He had been Royal's first sergeant back in the early days and had assumed the proportions of a father figure.

'No – don't talk to me about PCs – I've had 'em up to here,' he said, raising his hand to his throat. 'It's not the job I joined any more, not by a long chalk.'

'How long've we been friends Stan?' Royal asked, leaning against the filing cabinet. 'Best part of 15 years?'

'Give or take,' Ogwill agreed.

'I thought so,' Royal said, wrinkling his nose.

'Is that what you came over here for,' Ogwill said, 'to remind me how long we've been mates?'

'No. To tell you about this diabolical stroke they're pulling on me, Stan, so I can make sure it's really happening and I didn't just dream the whole thing.'

'Everybody pulls a diabolical stroke sometime,' Ogwill observed sagely.

'This is *double* diabolical,' Royal insisted. 'You wouldn't believe it.'

'Try me.'

'You know this Eastgate job I'm on?'

'Sure, I fixed up the PM, remember?'

'Well did you see Rivers on the TV the other night?'

'Was that the one where they had this nutter on who believed he was the spirit of some Indian chief?'

'Geronimo,' Royal said.

'That's it, and Rivers said he'd talk to anyone. . . .'

'Even the Great White Spirit,' Royal interrupted.

'. . . about psychic phenomena and all that junk.'

'You saw it then!'

Ogwill shook his head. 'No – I heard about it though. Sounded like Jack the Zipper's shot his bolt.'

Royal groaned. 'Well ever since then we've had every nutter and weirdie in Christendom on the blower, just itching to get in on the act.'

'Serves him right,' Ogwill said, 'he laid himself wide open so I heard.'

'Not him,' Royal exclaimed 'ME! That's what I'm telling you Stan. They've lumbered me with a psychic squad, every nutter who crawled out of the woodwork.'

'Now that is diabolical,' Ogwill said, shaking his head.

'That's what I thought.'

'You thought right, Bert.'

'So I need some good advice Stan – what d'you think?'

Ogwill pondered the question for a moment. 'Trust in the law,' he said firmly. 'That's what I always say – trust in the law to see you through. That's the trouble with the kids we're getting in the force these days – no stomach for the job. Keeled over the minute the knife went in. No, I tell you Bert – if you want my advice, trust in the law. Hold on to that and you'll come through.'

In the meditative silence that followed, Royal could hear the sounds of the pathologist muttering into his tape recorder, the voice growing louder as the quietude deepened, and then another background noise intruded, Mallow experimenting with a fresh tune on his harmonica.

Ogwill leaned forward and patted his knee. 'Trust in the law, Bert,' he said.

'Thanks Stan,' Royal replied miserably.

'You want one of these doughnuts – apple or jam?'

Royal shook his head.

* * *

Of course the psychic squad was merely a police euphemism for all the nuts, cranks, and weirdies who came chomping out of the undergrowth following Jack Rivers' unfortunate slip of the tongue during his address to the nation on TV. The police mind, while identifying nuts, cranks and weirdies as separate entities, had a penchant for the collective term and pretty well everything boiled down to a squad of one complexion or another. There were burglary squads, fraud squads, drugs squads, vice squads, porn squads, stolen car squads and even squads which begat squads. The squad syndrome was all part of the police machismo. A detective who didn't belong to one squad or another hadn't arrived.

The psychic squad, however, was merely a device to get around the embarrassment of the sackfulls of letters that had been arriving at the incident room ever since Rivers let it be known to four million viewers that the police were prepared to consider even the most unorthodox suggestions in the Eastgate murder. As the press took up the chant, it was decided at the highest level that the force should capitalise on this development with an imaginative open-handed response to the clamour from the psychic lobby. But not too imaginative or too open-handed, in fact just a once and for all gesture calculated to satisfy the psychics and get Jack Rivers off the hook. A two-day investigation was planned and so Bert Royal was given the dubious honour of leading the psychic squad.

They assembled at 10 o'clock in the morning at Eastgate police station where the incident room had been set up. The station was a decrepit red brick building ingrained with grime and soot. Its rooms and corridors were dingy musty places and the institutional brown colour scheme was mottled with damp and age. Bert Royal met them in the parade room, having taken the precaution of chewing a couple of Neutradonna tablets beforehand. He had feared something bizarre but the group awaiting him in eager anticipation out-stripped even his wildest nightmares.

He was propelled into the room by Jack Rivers who introduced himself with a sickly grin and then shouting to make himself heard above the clamour of voices, announced: 'I want to thank you all for taking the trouble to help us like this. . . .' He seized Royal by the arm and produced him rather like a trial exhibit. '. . . Detective Inspector Royal is your liaison officer – feel free to ask his help and advice. He will give you his undivided attention. Once again, we're very grateful to you all.' And with that he fled, leaving Royal to his destiny.

'I thought . . .' Bert Royal began, but his voice came out so gruffly that he cleared his throat and started again. 'I thought we'd take a trip around the principal locations of the inquiry, just so you could get the feel of the place and then we'll see the incident room, leaving tomorrow free for discussion and comment.' Without waiting for a reply he ushered them outside to a waiting personnel carrier and when they were all seated, he told the driver to move off.

The bus began a slow circumnavigation of Eastgate, slowing

down and stopping whenever Royal instructed. During the journey the DI kept up a running commentary. They rolled to a halt as Royal explained: 'This was where the girl was last seen alive. She was walking down this road and we believe that it was here that the events began which led to her death. If you'd like to get out now and . . . .' Royal had to sidestep swiftly from the aisle or he might have been trampled in the rush. His ulcer began to throb rhythmically.

When he stepped down from the bus he found one of the group lying on the pavement. It was the man with wild red hair who had appeared with Rivers on the television programme. He had a ribbon around his head holding a single feather and he was lying on his back close to the gutter with his arms folded across his chest. As he lay there passing traffic splashed him from nearby puddles.

'Is he all right?' Royal asked an elderly man with a grey beard who seemed to be the natural leader of the group.

'Oh yes – he's making contact.'

'Contact? With whom?'

'Geronimo.'

'I should've guessed.'

'You see, he believes he is the reincarnation of the great white spirit. He's reaching out to his ancestors.'

A bus passed close by spraying the prostrate figure with muddy water. Royal studied the face of the old man. He had bright blue eyes which twinkled with hidden humour, and his goatee beard was neatly trimmed. He had to be 70 years old, but at least he looked capable of some conversation.

'You don't believe that, do you?' Royal asked, wrinkling his nose.

The old man shrugged. 'Who knows,' he said, and he extended his hand. 'I'm Dr Engels, Raymond Engels from the Institute of Psychic Research.'

Royal took the handshake. 'That's the silliest thing I ever saw,' he nodded, 'lying there getting splashed by the traffic.'

Engels shrugged again: 'We each have our own technique. Personally I don't favour histrionics of that kind.'

Royal frowned: 'What's your speciality, Doctor,' he inquired politely.

'Oh, academic largely these days,' Engels replied, 'I practised medicine once, more years ago than I care to remember, but it was the mysteries of life which finally claimed my attention. My interests lean towards paramedical theories, the reaches of the mind.'

'So what brings you here?' Royal asked. He was about to add, 'with this load of nutters', but he restrained himself.

'I am devoting what time I have left,' Engels said, 'to some research of mine into the doctrine of perpetual force.'

'Come again,' Royal asked.

The old man smiled. 'I believe there is a relationship between time and violence. Where the pattern of life is disturbed by inordinately violent acts the time sequence is altered. My hypothesis is that such fragments of extreme violence are trapped in a time warp, caught up in, what shall we say, nature's tape recorder, which can be replayed under certain circumstances. There are people who have glimpsed the scenes of battle years later or have witnessed atrocities of previous centuries, all well documented. I'm looking for a contemporary study. This case seemed appropriate.'

'That's too much for me,' Royal shook his head.

Engels took his hand. 'You don't care too much for all this mumbo jumbo, do you, Inspector?'

'Tell you the truth – no. I'm just a simple copper,' Royal replied surprising himself with his own candour.'

'But that's not the real problem is it?' Engels frowned. 'The real problem is here,' he released Royal's hand and touched the DI's abdomen at the precise point of the ulcer. 'And I feel I must advise you my friend, you don't have too much time in which to make your decision.'

Royal was too astonished to speak. By the time he had regained his voice the old man was gone and a woman in a yellow plastic mac was tugging at his arm.

'I have it under my coat,' she whispered fiercely.

'What?' Royal exclaimed, fighting back the sensation of slipping into a dream sequence.

'His face.'

'His face?'

'Yes – he knows.'

'He does?'

'Oh yes – he knows everything.'

'What?'

'I'll show you.'

She opened the macintosh and produced a roll of linoleum which she spread on the pavement. 'There's the answer – you see?'

Royal peered at the mottled greenish fabric. 'I don't understand.'

'The face – the face – look at the face!'

Royal's mind was whirling. When the old man had gripped his hand, when he had brushed his fingers across his stomach, it was as though a calming influence had swept through him – and the ulcer – the ulcer – for that moment, hadn't the pain disappeared completely? Could it have happened – had he imagined it? Wasn't it coincidence or . . . .

'Jesus Christ!' Royal exclaimed as the next thought struck him.

'Yes – yes!' The woman shrieked, pointing at the piece of linoleum. 'You see him too!'

Royal tore himself away. He couldn't find Engels anywhere. The man lying on the pavement had begun to make a low moaning sound, beating his chest with his fists. A crowd of curious onlookers was beginning to gather. Over on the far side of the group Royal caught sight of a girl he had seen with Engels. She was standing a little apart from the others pushing wayward strands of hair under a floppy cap and clutching a large notebook. As Royal made his way towards her he could see that she was quite attractive in a studious sort of way.

'Excuse me,' he bagan, 'Aren't you with Dr Engels?'

'Yes – in a manner of speaking,' she said, 'Actually I'm at the university but I'm helping him out.' She flourished the pad. 'Taking notes, that sort of thing.'

'Look – I was just talking to him, he was telling me about his research,'

IS THERE A LITTLE PROBLEM DOWN HERE?
ULCER DETECTOR
SLOW
NUTTERS AT WORK

'Oh it's fascinating,' the girl said.

'He told me he was working on – oh what was the word – yes, paramedical, that's it.'

'That's right,' the girl said. 'He's a great man you know, in his field that is.'

'Paramedical?'

'Psychotherapy.'

'Psychotherapy?'

The girl smiled. 'You probably wouldn't know it, but he's one of the world's authorities on the subject.'

'What's it mean?' Royal asked.

'Well don't tell him I told you because he hates the term, but he's probably the greatest faith healer there ever was – he's done some fantastic things – really fantastic.'

Royal felt his mind reel again, but before he could get a grip on himself the man with the wild red hair encircled by the Indian headband let out a bloodcurdling moan from his prone position on the pavement. A shaggy mongrel ambled over and sniffed him.

'They generally come from the East you know.'

Royal swung around. The speaker was a young fellow in a gaudy anorak who was wearing padded earphones which sprouted antennae. A curly wire looped down to what looked like a small vacuum cleaner. The young man waggled the nozzle this way and that and has he did so the machine emitted a sporadic buzzing noise. He held one of the earphones away from his head.

'Yes – from the East usually,' he informed Royal. 'I thought you ought to know.'

The DI frowned. 'Who come from the East?'

But the padded earphone was back in place and the wearer was squinting in concentration. The antennae waggled and the vacuum cleaner buzzed once or twice.

'Who come from the East!' Royal shouted.

The young fellow lifted the earphone again. 'I can't hear you with these on,' he said.

'Who come from the East?' Royal yelled. The relief had been short-lived, the ulcer was beginning to hurt again.

'You don't have to shout,' the young fellow protested and Royal lowered his voice.

'I didn't quite get it – who come from the East?'

'The ALF of course.'

'The ALF?'

The young fellow gave him a deprecating glance. 'Alien Life Form.'

'Oh – I see.'

'I'm a ufologist – you've heard of UFOs, I suppose?'

'Oh yes,' Royal said. 'Yes indeed.'

'We can pick up ALF vehicles with this equipment,' said the ufologist, 'mainly exhaust emissions, it's very exciting.'

'I'd never had guessed,' Royal said. 'Looks like a vacuum cleaner to me.'

'This,' said the ufologist in a mortified tone, 'is an atmos-megameter.' He waved the nozzle about inducing a little more buzzing. 'It's very sensitive.'

'What's it do? Royal asked.

'The atmos-megameter,' said the ufologist proudly, 'can detect any trace of a UFO. In the States you know, they fitted them to police cars until two patrolmen were kidnapped by the ALF in Kentucky. It's dangerous work. You have to be alert all the time.'

'I can imagine,' Royal said sceptically.

'Oh yes indeed,' repeated the ufologist, 'lower your guard for a second and they'll get you.'

'The ALF,' Royal said.

'That's right – most of your unsolved crime is the work of the aliens, you know that don't you?'

'Is that a fact?' Royal said with a straight face. 'So you reckon we've got to stop nicking villains and go for the little green men from Mars?' But his sarcasm was lost on the ufologist who had replaced his earphones and was once more intent on picking up the whisper of extra-terrestial skullduggery. The small vacuum cleaner buzzed curtly.

Royal moved away. He couldn't see Dr Engels anywhere and now quite a crowd had gathered, attracted by the antics of the psychic squad. Perhaps it hadn't been such a good idea to let them off the bus after all. Suddenly the red haired man leaped up from the pavement.

'Uh – wee – unger – wee – chung – eye – soon,' he began to chant, hopping from foot to foot. The onlookers became restless and moved forward.

'OK – everybody back on the bus', Royal ordered, anxious to head off trouble. He had to shout to make himself heard. 'Back on the bus – we're moving on.'

When he had managed to herd them all onto the personnel carrier Royal continued the conducted tour, identifying the landmarks as they cruised past, slowing down in a street where a task force team was engaged on house-to-house inquiries, to offer a brief description of this basic investigation technique, then on to the spot where the girl's body was found. Once again the psychic squad alighted and milled around. All except the mud-spattered Indian chief who was so exhausted from his previous exertions that he had fallen asleep across the back seat. An intense woman with a stone on a silver chain insisted on dangling the talisman over the exact spot where the body had been found. A strange man in a wollen hat whose spectacles were held together with elastoplast, became so excited that he collapsed and had to be revived by artificial respiration.

Royal looked for Dr Engels, but the psychotherapist was nowhere to be found and the DI began to wonder whether he had imagined the soothing interlude. His stomach was hurting him again. And by the time they returned to the police station Bert Royal's nerves were badly frayed once more. It was a blessed relief to wheel them into the incident room and briefly explain the procedures of statement taking and cross indexing. He was back on safe familiar ground and even the old-fashioned glances from the duty shift didn't perturb him unduly. When they broke up for the day Royal sought out the girl with the notepad and said as off-handedly as he could muster: 'I didn't see Dr Engels again.'

'No,' the girl said. 'He had to leave. He's an old man and he tires easily.' She gnawed the end of her pencil. 'It's funny though, he seemed quite concerned about something.'

'The thing that puzzles me,' Royal said, 'is if he's as clued-up as you say – why's he here with this mob?'

The girl laughed: 'Oh you've got it all wrong,' she said. 'Dr Engels isn't *with* these other people – he's observing them – it's part of his study.'

* * *

Next morning the gnome-like doctor with the grey beard and enigmatic expression was back again. It was grandstand day when the psychic squad pooled its ideas with the intentions of coming up with a solution to the murder. A researcher from *Psychic News* came along with a tape recorder. Oh yes – it was a big day, vindication day, and what's more, it was being recorded for posterity. With all the excitement and sense of occasion, Bert Royal had little difficulty in slipping away with Dr Engels who accepted his invitation to step into another office for a few moments' rest. They left the experts in the parade room, poring over maps and jabbering eagerly into the tape recorder, competing with each other for a share of the limelight.

With the inbred cunning of his many years as a detective, Royal approached the purpose of his diversion circuitously.

'You know Doctor,' he began, 'you interest me quite a bit.'

Engels sat down. he looked drawn and exhausted, but his eyes twinkled with inner amusement. 'Is that so, inspector.'

'Oh yes,' Royal said. 'I get the impression that there's more to you than meets the eye.'

'Isn't that true of all of us?'

'But you especially.'

Engels folded his hands. 'You mean because I happen to know that you my friend have a stomach ulcer which may perforate at any time and that you are unable to come to terms with your medical advice.'

Royal smiled: 'Since you put it that way – yes, that's exactly it.'

'You're not unique,' Engels said, 'You're not even an unusual case. Forgive me if I'm blunt, but when you reach my age you also will discover that the niceties of polite conversation merely waste valuable time. As I said, you are a common example of the age, inspector, the thing I find so interesting as an observer is a detective, a man of action, a folk hero figure perhaps, so wracked with self doubt. I find that phenomenon quite fascinating. So – I have been frank with you, now you must do me the same courtesy. What is it you want of me?'

Royal frowned: 'All I know is that yesterday when I was in your company, the pain went away. For the first time in two years I wasn't worrying myself sick on that score. Now that's pretty remarkable even for a hairy old copper like me to swallow. So I made some inquiries about you Doctor and I understand everything I was told. I can't entirely believe it, but at least I'm willing to try.'

Engels said: 'Speak plainly my friend. Don't try to justify yourself, it isn't necessary.'

'Well then,' Royal went on, 'what I suppose I really want to know is . . . are you as good as your reputation?'

'Better,' Engels said, without any hint of boastfulness, 'far better.'

Then the other question is the jackpot – can you cure me?'

Engels laughed. 'If I had a pound note for every time I have been asked that question I would be a rich man.'

Royal's expression began to stiffen at the apparent rebuff, but Engels held up a hand. 'Come now – not so sensitive – I'm merely saying that there is no simple answer to your question. I cannot work miracles if that's what you mean. I cannot cure you either by the pressure of the hand or some incantation. But you can cure yourself, of that I am certain, and if you wish I can show you the way.'

'Doctor,' Royal interrupted, 'if you're trying to let me down lightly. . . .'

'Be patient,' Engels said. 'Let me explain. When I was a boy in Cambridge and later in medical school, certain effects occured around me. Furniture would move, desks and beds and laboratory equipment would move around because of my presence. I discovered that I had the mental ability to . . . what shall I say . . . adjust my surroundings. But this is no special gift. No divine power. It is merely an example of the potential of the brain my friend. You know the average person uses less than 10 per cent of the brain's capacity. I merely discovered the ability to develop a little further down the road of evolution. In the middle ages I would have been burned at the stake,' he chuckled at the thought. 'In reality I was merely regarded as an oddity by my contemporaries. Compared with the marvels of science I was just a circus act.'

Royal made to interrupt but Engels raised his hand again. 'Please allow me to finish. These days I find questions particularly tiring. Let me give you an example, inspector; this case of yours interests me, the doctrine of perpetual force. If I were to say to you that I can see that girl at the precise moment of her death, recapture that moment by intercepting the residue of violence which remains trapped in time, you would not believe me. If I could place my hand on the perpetrator's shoulder and offer positive proof, then perhaps, but the experience of the mind is not like that, proof is elusive, and I am no match for the natural sceptism of my fellow men. But I see that death scene as plainly as I see you. Or rather, I experience it.'

Royal said: 'Doctor Engels, I've spent the best part of my life dealing in facts, it's hard to accept. . . .'

Engels placed a finger on his lips commanding silence. 'But with you, inspector,' he went on, 'I have an opportunity to prove my words. Give me your hand.'

Obediently Royal offered his hand and Engels took it in a warm dry grasp. The detective felt his anxiety slip away. The ulcer ceased to trouble him. A sense of well-being enveloped him.

'You see,' Engels said, 'I am freeing your brain from the limitations you choose to impose upon it. To give you an easy analogy – like jump leads from a battery.'

'I don't understand,' Royal said helplessly. 'I know what I feel but I don't understand. Are you curing me?'

Engels shook his head. 'No,' he said, 'I'm helping you to cure yourself.'

'Then what should I do?'

Engels said: 'I can only offer you a suggestion. The decision must be yours.'

'What suggestion?'

'Let me say this. The vibrations of your mind reveal tension, great tension, first you must reverse the process.'

'How – how should I do that?'

'You must cease to be a policeman.'

'But the job's all I've ever known – what should I do?'

'You are a severe case of occupational anxiety. You are psychologically unsuited to your work, it's common enough. Most times there are compensating features, but you have pushed yourself too far. Your chronic condition requires drastic remedy. First you must seek solace in tranquility.'

'Where would I find it?' Royal asked, his hand still held in the warm soothing grip.

'In flowers,' Engels replied simply. 'The great healing properties of photosynthesis have yet to be discovered. You must work with plants and draw nourishment from the sun. You must learn to photosynthesise.'

'I don't understand,' Royal blurted out and Engels released his hand.

The doctor's face was very pale and his eyes were closed. 'There,' he said, his voice little more than a whisper, 'now you are disappointed. you really expected a miracle.'

'Doctor Engels,' Royal said, screwing up his face in concentration, 'it's hard for me to grasp, give me time.'

'I have no time,' Engels said.

'But I don't know anything about flowers,' Royal said.

'Then you must learn,' Engels said simply.

'Will you help me?'

'Perhaps,' Engels said, 'Now I am very tired. You must let me rest.'

'But what must I do first?' Royal persisted.

'The first step is the hardest of all,' Engels said, his eyes still closed. 'First you must believe.'

* * *

The report Bert Royal wrote on the psychic squad operation

was a masterpiece; there was no doubt about that. Brian Webber read it through a second time with mounting admiration. It was concise and to the point, no pertinent detail had been left out, it had been carefully documented, indexed and minuted. In its crisp manilla folder the report had progressed through the hierarchy to the chief's office with suitable comments added at each stage culminating in a flourish of praise from the chief. Now it was on the downward journey back along the chain of command to the author. The report had dropped into Brian Webber's basket that morning and the DCI, reading it through for a third time, found his admiration undiminished. It was a minor classic in the annals of police writing, a work of perfection in every sense. The fact that the contents of the report were complete gibberish did nothing to detract from that perfection.

Webber picked up the report and went down to the DI's office. He found Royal at his desk studying a newspaper which he pushed aside as Webber entered.

'Nice piece of work Bert.' Webber said, dropping the report on the desk. 'Nice bouquet from the chief too. Did you a bit of good, I wouldn't be at all surprised.'

Royal smiled. He was chewing Neutradonna and his lips were specked with fragments of the white tablets.

'Oh yes, I've got to hand it to you,' Webber said, fascinated by the white-flecked lips, 'you've certainly got the gift when it comes to putting a report together. I hear they're very pleased with the way you handled that psychic squad up at headquarters. A nice smooth cosmetic operation. Feather in your cap I'd say Bert.'

Royal continued to smile.

'Look Bert,' Webber continued. 'I didn't have a chance to ask you before, not just between the two of us. What'd you think of the psychic squad?'

'Nutters,' Royal replied flatly, 'Grade A.'

'Oh come on,' Webber said, fishing for a conversational advantage, 'I heard you were pretty thick with that old geezer – what's his name – Dr Engels. What about him?'

'Mad as a nit,' Royal said.

'Well the chief was impressed,' Webber went on, 'and that's what counts. You get good vibes there all right. In fact if I were you . . . I mean if you want my advice. . . I'd put in for the next promotion board on the strength of this Bert,' he tapped the report with a forefinger, 'strike while the iron's hot.'

'Tell you the truth, guvnor,' Royal said, in a disinterested way, 'I'm thinking of putting my ticket in.'

'Jack in the job!' Webber voiced his surprise. 'That's not your style Bert. I always thought you'd got the job right under your skin. Jack it in for what?'

'Oh I dunno,' Royal said, 'but there's nothing here for me any more.'

'Had an offer, eh?' Webber tried to interpret the DI's mood. 'Don't tell me . . . security officer at Boots, or is it that cushy number at the Gas Board?'

'Nothing certain,' Royal sidestepped the question.

'Or that insurance lark?'

Royal shook his head.

'Carter didn't talk you into that water bailiff thing, did he?'

Royal got up: 'Excuse me guv,' he said, 'I'm late already for the shift change in the incident room. No sense in blotting my copybook now.'

As he went out of the door Webber called after him: 'Bert you're nuts – here's the chief eating out've your hand, for Godsake!'

But Bert Royal had gone and so Brian Webber picked up the psychic squad report and placed it carefully in the DI's wire tray. As he did so he couldn't help noticing the newspapers Royal had left behind. It was the local rag and as he picked it up out of idle curiosity, he was greeted by a picture of Tony Mallow grinning from ear to ear over the caption: 'Morgue PC vies for Euro-song fame'. He turned the paper over the classifieds and saw that one of the job ads had been ringed in black crayon. It said: 'Gardener wanted – no experience required'.

Thirteen The Inspection

THEY sat naked in the sauna room of the headquarters sports complex, Sir Ralph Hawk reclining comfortably on his bath towel, hands clasped across a small pot belly; Henry Grey squatting on the low slatted bench beside the HMI, perspiring freely in the steamy atmosphere and looking rather insignificant without the trappings of his immaculate uniform. Sir Ralph was staring at the ceiling and Grey, globules of moisture beading his toothbrush moustache, was trying hard to suppress the wheezing sound which threated to escape from his lungs and thereby reveal his state of complete exhaustion.

When the HMI had suggested a game of squash upon their return from S Division, Henry Grey who fancied himself as something of an afficianado had diplomatically vowed to allow the HMI to win by a narrow margin. In his crisp white shorts and vest he walked into the court with a small superior smile hovering on his lips. In the event, his determination to allow Sir Ralph the edge evaporated almost immediately as to Grey's astonishment the HMI played like a dervish, wacking the ball around the court with such ferocity that the deputy chief was soundly thrashed.

Now Grey silently nursed his resentment as he tried in vain to calm his thumping heart and adjust the double vision that had plagued him ever since one of Sir Ralph's particularly forceful shots had struck him on the temple.

'Good old British know-how Henry,' said the HMI with his usual penchant for starting a conversation with a baffling non-sequitur, 'that's the ticket, nothing to beat the old British brain box.' Sir Ralph's words floated up towards the ceiling, muffled by the steam.

'Oh absolutely Sir Ralph,' Grey replied, finding it infuriatingly difficult to concentrate with two images of the HMI shimmering before his eyes.

'Take the British Bobby,' Sir Ralph went on. 'Envy of the world. Look at Europe, your CRS, your Bundesgrenschutz, can't hold a candle to the British Bobby with his boots blacked and buttons polished. And you know why, Henry?'

Grey hadn't the faintest idea. He tried blinking rapidly but that didn't seem to help. The two Sir Ralphs still had him at a disadvantage.

The HMI tapped his temple: 'British know-how, that's why.' Pivoting on an elbow, Sir Ralph turned to regard Grey keenly: 'And they're all clamouring for it Henry, you can take my word for that. The Yanks, the Aussies, Germans, Japs, third world. That's the place to make a name for yourself these days Henry – out there.'

Grey tried holding his nose and blowing against the pressure, but the two Sir Ralphs maddeningly refused to merge. 'Out where, Sir Ralph?'

'Don't be obtuse Henry,' the HMI replied settling back again, this time clasping his hands behind his head. 'Out there in the world. Time to broaden the old horizons. Nut much left in this country anyway, too claustrophobic.'

'I don't quite get the drift, Sir Ralph,' Grey replied, wiggling his eyebrows desperately.

'Not much scope for ambition is what I mean.'

'Oh I wouldn't say that.'

The HMI smiled. 'How many times you have been short-listed Henry?'

'Oh er – once or twice. . . .'

'Six to be precise,' said the HMI flatly, 'and passed over every time.'

Grey was flustered, he felt his perspiring face begin to flush. Of course within the HMI's Home Office circles, his career details would be an open book. 'But what I meant Sir Ralph was. . . .'

The HMI cut him short. 'What you meant Henry is that every time you apply for the top job you get pipped at the post by some bright young bugger with a head stuffed full of fancy notions. The wind of change is blowing Henry,' he disengaged a hand and wagged a finger portentiously, 'and sometimes it blows exceeding chill.'

'Does that mean,' said Grey glumly, for he had a healthy respect for the HMI's analysis of the current political mood within the service, 'that I'm over the hill so to speak, Sir Ralph?'

The HMI swung his legs to the ground and leaned forward clutching bony knee caps. 'Not at all Henry, what it means is it's time to grasp the nettle, make the break, take the old plunge.'

'But where,' Grey exclaimed, 'and how?'

'That's what I've been telling you,' replied Sir Ralph with a grandiose sweep of the arm. 'Out there Henry, new horizons, pack the old bag and take off. The world's your oyster.'

'Oh I see,' cried Henry Grey caught up by Sir Ralph Hawks's enthusiam. 'I see – I see.' And he really did see. Miraculously the HMI had clicked back into perfect vision. Who could have asked for a better omen.

'Capital Henry,' said Sir Ralph, slapping Grey's shoulder wetly. 'Matter of fact I may be able to do you a bit of a favour old man, strictly on the QT of course.' He leaned forward in a confidential manner: 'Friend of mine at the FO, sound chap from the old regiment, straight as a die, well he was telling me they've got some contracts open for senior police advisors, top drawer stuff. Government level, free hand, all that sort of thing. Asked me if I'd keep a weather eye open. Nod's as good as a wink, eh Henry.'

Grey nodded his agreement. Where the HMI was concerned, a nod was definitely as good as a wink. 'To a blind horse, eh Sir Ralph,' he forced a laugh.

'A what?'

'A blind horse,' Grey explained, 'A nod's as good as a wink to a blind horse.'

'Don't be ridiculous,' said the HMI, 'it's got nothing to do with horses. This is good practical policemanship, a chance to show 'em what you're made of Henry.'

'Where exactly, Sir Ralph?' Grey asked, the HMI's gesture conjuring up pictures of exotic places.

'Take your pick,' said Sir Ralph expansively. 'How about El Salvador. Full of Latin American promise, dusky maidens, that sort of thing.' The HMI winked knowingly.

'I thought they kidnapped Europeans there,' Grey replied

hesitantly, dredging up snippets of information from his memory, 'then tortured them to death and dumped their bodies in alleyways daubed with political slogans.'

'A temporary setback that's all,' said the HMI, breezily. 'But what a challenge eh. Show 'em what the British Bobbies are made of.'

Looking down at his own pink flesh, Henry Grey was reminded of the precise composition of his body. He imagined it riddled with machine gun bullets.

'How about Sierra Leone then?' asked Sir Ralph.

'Don't they call that the white man's grave?' Grey inquired as the erotic images of dancing girls gave way to an impression of disease ridden jungle.

'Nonsense,' contradicted the HMI, 'Nothing good old British stamina can't take care of.'

'Perhaps somewhere a little more civilised,' said Grey hesistantly, for he didn't want to offend Sir Ralph.

'Uganda,' said the HMI.

'Surely we don't send people *there*?' Grey blurted out.

The HMI tapped the side of his nose. 'Need to know only Henry,' he said, 'Beautiful climate, charming people.'

'Isn't there anywhere,' Grey began rummaging around in his distinctly rusty recollection of geography, 'a little closer to home?'

'Well they're hardly likely to send you to the Isle of Wight, are they?'

Grey looked crestfallen. 'It's just that I don't seem to get on too well with foreigners Sir Ralph. Odd sort of fellows. We had a superintendent from Pakistan down on the computer management course, complaining that they didn't even have telephones in Pakistan. Had the dickens of a game convincing him it was all worthwhile.'

'No imagination,' said Sir Ralph shaking his head, 'see what happens when we abandon these countries to their own devices. Morale goes for a burton. That's why they still need good men Henry, men like you.'

'Well I wouldn't mind giving it a try,' Grey said, 'but it always seems so . . . well . . . so precarious.'

'Trouble with you Henry,' said the HMI, 'is you believe everything you read in the newspapers. No more dodgy than crossing Hyde Park on a Sunday afternoon, not when you're British.'

'I wouldn't mind Hong Kong,' Grey brightened up, but the HMI shook his head.

'Colonial types have got it all sewn up and good luck to 'em I say. Treacherous little devils the Chinese.'

They sat in silence for a moment and then Sir Ralph Hawk snapped his fingers as a new thought occurred to him. 'I've got it Henry – St Helena – suit you down to the ground.'

The proposition was just too much for Grey's dim memory of his schoolboy atlas. 'I can't quite place St Helena, Sir Ralph,' he said, trying hard not to reveal his ignorance.

'Down in the South Atlantic, Henry,' replied the HMI firmly, airing his knowledge, 'and still under the old UK wing. Ceded to us in 1834.'

'That sounds more like it,' Grey replied more cheerfully. The initials UK still inspired confidence, and the UK would most certainly have washed its hands of anywhere with an inhospitable climate or primitive table manners. Besides, St Helena was a good dependable sort of name that could be pronounced easily without affecting one of those poncey foreign accents. It all sounded eminently British. 'Wouldn't mind having a crack at that one, Sir Ralph.'

'Excellent,' said the HMI rising swiftly and wrapping the bath towel around him in the manner of a toga. 'I'll put your name up then, Henry. Write you a letter of recommendation myself.'

'Would you really? That's most decent of you, Sir Ralph,' Grey oozed gratitude. 'You're right you know – I am beginning to stagnate a bit.'

'New lease of life Henry,' boomed the HMI, 'just what the doctor ordered.'

Grey became so effusive that Sir Ralph hadn't the heart to explain that the little dot on the map a thousand miles off West Africa which had been exploited for 150 years by the East India Company hardly came up to Grey's vision of utopia. For

... ON ST HELENA YOU WOULD BE FOLLOWING IN THE FOOTSTEPS OF THE OTHER GREAT MEN THAT ENGLAND HAS SENT THERE, LIKE NAPOLEON......

survival they relied on a £4 million hand out from Whitehall and their flax industry had taken a nose dive ever since the Post Office switched from string to synthetics to tie up parcels. The social highlight was an occasional visit from a British supply ship.

'Sundowners on the terrace, eh Sir Ralph,' Grey romanticised.

'Oh I dare say,' the HMI replied, 'I dare say.' He was reminded of the conversation with his Foreign Office acquaintance over a couple of pinkies at Boodles.

'What would they want a police adviser for?' Sir Ralph had asked.

'Head man's a status freak,' the FO official had replied with a nervous twitch, 'Got to find somebody for the Godforsaken place just to shut him up. See what you can do Ralphy eh?'

'Peach groves and orange blossom,' Grey prattled on excitedly, mentally discarding his inhibitions at the prospect. 'Dark skinned girls with firm young breasts. . .'

He could hardly believe it was his own voice he was hearing. The exertion, the heat, dehydration, the promise of forbidden fruit had suddenly induced a feverish light-headedness, causing him to momentarily lose his rigid self-control. '. . . young muscular thighs . . . squeezing . . . squeezing . . .' he piped in a reedy voice, '. . . and buttocks, heaving buttocks . . . ahhhhh. . . .'

Sir Ralph Hawk took his arm and adopted a paternal tone of voice. 'I think that's enough excitement for one day, Henry,' he said, 'Time for a nice cold shower old man.'

And Grey, weakly babbling abject apologies, allowed the HMI to lead him out of the sauna, clutching his towel tightly around him in the hope that the physical manifestation of his erotic day-dream would pass unnoticed.

Fourteen Crime Intelligence

DETECTIVE Sergeant Victor Hardwick spent a great deal of his time raiding his brother-in-law's scrap metal yard. It was good solid CID work, the sort of thing he enjoyed, and so every now and then he would borrow a couple of DCs, a handful of uniform men and perhaps a dog handler for good measure, and they would roar down to the scrapyard in a convey of cars, headlights blazing, blue lights flashing, and turn the place over in fine old style. Over his 20 years in the job Hardwick had become a past master in the technique of raiding premises and every time he would burst into the caravan which served as an office, scowl menacingly and announce: 'OK everybody stay put – this is a police raid.' And Alex Donnelly, his brother-in-law, would look up from his desk with tired, patient eyes and reply: 'You got a warrant this time, Vic?' To which Hardwick would invariably respond: 'Since when did I need a warrant Alex – this is family business.' With a sigh Donnelly would push his work aside, slide across his scrap register for official scrutiny and exchange pleasantries on family affairs, while the raiding party scrambled over the acres of junk in the yard outside.

When it was all over, Hardwick would return to the station, de-brief his team and then write up the reports in meticulous detail. The S Division had never had a more conscientious crime intelligence officer than Victor Hardwick, and nobody seemed unduly concerned that all the intelligence contained in the CID index appeared to relate exclusively to the activities of Alex Donnelly's scrap metal business. Vic Hardwick could be relied upon for cast iron intelligence and that was all that really mattered.

Of course Hardwick's preoccupation with his brother-in-law's scrap yard was not as simple as might be apparent at face value. For one thing D/Sgt Victor Hardwick was blissfully ignorant of the fact that Donnelly really was a high-class villain and that was why he never complained to the brass about this seemingly unwarranted intrusion into his business. Similarly, Alex Donnelly, who felt quite confident in his ability to hoodwink his numbskull brother-in-law, was unaware of the fact that the S Division crime intelligence reports had been circulated to the regional crime squad where such painstaking and diligent CID work had been duly rewarded. In fact the squad had singled out Donnelly as a Zatopek target.

Alex Donnelly cut a fine figure for a scrap dealer with his penchant for pinstripe business suits, diamond tie tacks and smooth camel overcoats. His thick dark hair was greying at the temples adding a distinguished touch to his appearance and he would have passed in the city for a merchant banker or stockbroker, with his meticulous old-world manners and careful attention to the niceties of social etiquette. Nowadays he preferred to be described as a ferrous metal factor, a respectable description of his flourishing business exporting other people's antiques concealed in shipments of processed metal. He had built up a lucrative Euro-business on the continental metal exchange which qualified for all the Common Market subsidies, but to his criminal associates who specialised in plundering country mansions, Alex Donnelly was a 20 per cent of market value, take-it-or-leave-it fence and a leading light of their fraternity.

If only his waspish younger sister Mavis hadn't upped and married that pride of the local law, Vic Hardwick, the chain of events that eventually elevated Alex Donnelly to the exalted criminal rank of squad target might never have happened. But, as was his nature, he took the bumbling attentions of his detective brother-in-law philosophically and in the course of Hardwick's frequent visits to his yard, even found him a useful if unwitting, source of police information. While the raiding party rummaged half-heartedly through the mountains of twisted metal and gutted car shells, he would lubricate the conversation with Scotch and American sipped from cut glass tumblers in quite a convivial manner.

Compared with the fastidious Donnelly, Vic Hardwick was a shambling hulk of a man, his off-the-peg blue suit shiny at elbows and trouser seat, lapels ash stained from the ever present cigarette, shirt collar loosened around a bull neck which rose to a sloping head upon which Brylcreem-plastered hair gleamed like patent leather. For his bearlike frame Hardwick was hopelessly underpowered and could function effectively only in short bursts, frequently collapsing into the nearest chair to recharge his flagging energies. Quite what Mavis had seen in him, Donnelly was at a loss to comprehend. But despite their singular incompatibility things went tolerably well for quite a while as each man played his own game with the other.

Then as so often happens where so much has been invested in preserving the status quo, an unrelated event snuffs out the sun and changes everything forever. By a coincidence of geography, Alex Donnelly's scrapyard happened to be in Eastgate, sprawling across a vacant tract of wilderness beyond the high rise flats, once earmarked for a grandiose regional shopping complex, then abandoned as the civic planners fled before the hot breath of Eastgate's transplanted slum dwellers. And as any self-respecting villain will testify, there's nothing quite like a murder investigation for shaking the mice out of the woodwork. Soon after the discovery of the girl's body, Eastgate was crawling with detectives to the chagrin of the criminal fraternity who immediately began to batten down the hatches and prepare to weather the storm. But not before the house-to-house team had stumbled across an assortment of stolen colour TV sets in a lock-up garage, a cannabis cache hidden in a roof space, and a full kit of house-breaking implements lovingly concealed under a loose floorboard in someone's spare bedroom. Several of the boys found the frenzied police activity just too much for their blood pressure and took off for a belated holiday in Tenerife. Alex Donnelly declined a seat on the chartered jet. It would, he told his colleagues, take more than a two-penny-ha'penny murder to crack his nerve. Besides he was to all intents and purposes, a legitimate businessman and he had interests and reputation to protect.

At the same time, the first shock waves of the murder were buffeting the police ranks as the CID assembled en-masse for their conference with the appointed investigating officer in the person of Detective Superintendent Jack Rivers. Ladling the sarcasm as was expected of an ace sleuth from headquarters making a guest appearance in the sticks, Rivers briefed his teams; victim background, house-to-house, suspects, incident room, admin and support, search team liaison, scene-of-crime, and finally, his eyes roving across the assembly until he found the right face, crime intelligence.

'Crime intelligence,' said Jack Rivers, rolling the words around his tongue as though savouring a tasty morsel, 'Ah yes . . . Sergeant Hardwick. You want to give us the benefit of your vast experience?'

Hardwick blinked and a perplexed expression formed on his face. He cleared his throat and began leafing through a huge file of paperwork balanced on his knee.

'Yes sir,' he began hesistantly. 'Thank you sir, well sir, the criminal behavioural patterns of Eastgate fall into distinct categories which can best be enumerated if one divides the area into demographic sectors which can then be colour coded for spectral analysis. . . .'

'Well well,' Rivers smirked his delight at having discovered such a perfect foil for his acid wit. 'If we want a sociology lesson we'll know who to come to.' Then he was rewarded by a ripple of laughter and reminded himself that a good commander gets the best from his men by cultivating a sense of humour.

'Hardwick,' he purred, enjoying the moment. 'So you're the crime intelligence wizard, OK? Well, I want the lowdown on Eastgate and I want it fast – if that's all right with you that is . . . if you've got nothing more pressing to occupy your obviously considerable talents.'

'Yes sir . . . I mean, no sir,' Hardwick replied, enthusiastically, as Rivers' sarcasm passed over his head. 'Thank you, sir. . . .'

'And you can cut out all that pansy twaddle,' said Rivers, 'where'd you pick it up anyway?'

'Open University,' replied Hardwick proudly, 'I'm doing social studies, colour coded.'

With the valediction of his chief still ringing in his ears, Vic Hardwick determined to put his resolve into practice the best

THEY ARE NOT AS BAD AS
THE ONE'S I'VE JUST SEEN
OF THE CHIEF SUPER

way he knew how. The pressure was on; it was time for vision, daring, and dynamic action. He vowed to raid his brother-in-law's scrap yard every day . . . starting right now. Hardwick strode purposefully out of the conference and went upstairs to collect his coat. As he walked into his office he found one of his old cronies from the crime squad sitting on his desk and smoking a Corona Corona which Hardwick had kept in his in-tray since Christmas.

'Hey Vic,' the DC greeted him him with easy familiarity. They used to play poker together back in their singlemen's days. 'I was just passing so I thought I'd drop in, sort of on the QT as you're an old mate, and let you have a gander at these.' He spread a selection of photographs across the desk. Hardwick stared at them in stunned silence. They were shots of Donnelly's scrap yard. 'This one in particular,' said the DC, dropping ash from the purloined cigar onto the blotter as he slid the last picture across the desk. It was a close-up of Hardwick himself coming out of the caravan which served as an office.

'What's all this Jack?' Hardwick wanted to know, blinking in surprise and the detective winked conspiratorially.

'Just thought a word to the wise Vic. My gaffer'd crucify me if he knew I was telling you this, but that's what mates are for eh? It'd be a poor old world if we couldn't help each other out.'

'That's me on there!' Hardwick yelped. 'What the hell's going on?'

'Alex Donnelly,' the DC confided, leaning forward.

'Alex Donnelly?' echoed Hardwick, his voice rising in alarm.

'Shh, not so loud.'

'What about Alex Donnelly?' Hardwick asked in a hoarse whisper.

'That's what I'm telling you,' said the DC, 'he's a squad target.'

'What!'

'Twenty-four hour surveillance.'

'What for?' Hardwick put the question desperately.

'Zatopek,' the DC told him.

'Jesus,' Hardwick breathed the word. It didn't bear thinking about.

'Just a word to the wise Vic,' the DC counselled with a wink as he slid off the desk and dropped the cigar into the wastepaper basket. 'Oh and you know what the squad's like – need to know only – all that caper. So I was never here Vic, OK? If anyone should ask, you haven't seen me in years.'

He spirited the pictures into an inside pocket, slid out of the door and disappeared before the incredulous Hardwick could question him further.

With a low moan Vic Hardwick slumped into his chair suddenly weak at the knees, his mind reeling. Alex Donnelly, his brother-in-law, a Zatopek target! It wasn't possible. Had he dreamed it? Had it been some apparition there in his office? Some quirk of his over-heated imagination? Hardwick rubbed his eyes. Yes – that must be it, the excitement of his own contribution to the murder briefing was playing tricks on him. Mavis's brother a squad target? It wasn't possible. He must have been dreaming. Hardwick wrinkled his nose. What was that smell? Something burning! His eyes fell on the wastepaper basket from which blue smoke was curling.

* * *

'My God Alex,' Hardwick told Donnelly as he sidled into the caravan which served as an office, coat collar turned up, face hidden under a cloth cap and muffler in the hope of keeping his true identity from the prying long toms of the crime squad. 'You've made a right monkey out've me.'

Donnelly who was in his customary place behind his desk, sighed and pushed his paperwork away. His brother-in-law's pained expression, odd appearance and injured tone, seemed to indicate a prolonged session.

'You don't look so good Vic,' he replied mildly, 'you'd better sit down.'

Hardwick flopped heavily into a chair. After extinguishing

the fire in his wastepaper basket he had headed directly for the scrap yard to have it out with Donnelly.

'You've made me look a right mug,' he complained accusingly.

'Vic,' Donnelly said patiently, 'I haven't the faintest idea what you're talking about.'

'And what's Mavis going to say, eh?' Hardwick grumbled. 'Answer me that?'

'Look,' Donnelly remained unruffled. 'You've got the advantage on me. What am I supposed to have done?'

'All this time and you didn't even tell me . . . ME, your own brother-in-law. You just let me keep on coming here without so much as a nod or a wink. It really is too bad Alex.'

Donnelly leaned forward resting his elbows on the desk and asked gently. 'What's too bad Vic?'

'And to think I had to find out for myself.'

'Find out what Vic?'

'That you're a squad target – that's what! That there's Ds up telegraph poles, in butchers' vans, and pretending to dig up the road, taking pictures of everything that moves around here including ME!'

Alex Donnelly sat up and devoted a second or two to controlling his facial muscles. 'A squad target eh?' he mused, shifting his mind into overdrive to assess the ramifications of this piece of information.

'A Zatopek target,' Hardwick scowled miserably, 'the one that goes the distance.'

Careful to avoid betraying a hint of emotion Donnelly asked: 'How did you find out?'

'From the horse's mouth,' Hardwick replied, 'from the squad itself. And how d'you think that makes me feel? My own brother-in-law a squad target and I'm the last one to find out. I'm telling you Alex, you've made a right monkey out've me and no mistake. What's Mavis going to say?'

'You haven't told her then,' Donnelly inquired, merely to keep the conversation going although he really couldn't have cared less about his sister's opinion at this juncture. He had enough to worry about himself.

'Of course not – I only just found out myself and I came straight over. You've spoiled everything Alex, you know that don't you? I was going to do a raid to day and another tomorrow. I'm on this murder team you know, and we're pulling out all the stops. It was my big chance, but how can I do it now with those buggers from the squad perched all around. You've queered my pitch good and proper.'

They talked on in this fashion a while longer, Hardwick accusing, Donnelly placating as he extracted more and more information from his brother-in-law. The picture certainly looked gloomy, but he was a resilient and resourceful villain and now that the first flush of shock had passed, he began to examine the problem with a cool and analytical approach. There had to be a way out if only he could figure it out.

The more Donnelly thought about it, the more he pinpointed the murder inquiry as being worthy of consideration. Here was a single event stirring everything up, exciting the forces of law and order, turning a dammed great searchlight on the shady areas of Eastgate. It was of constant amazement to a realist like himself that an otherwise historically acceptable facet of human behaviour, the taking of life, could still cause such an uproar. People were getting knocked off every day; in car crashes; through the bumbling inefficiency of bureaucracy; at the hands of the medical profession, and nobody so much as raised an eyebrow. But that, he accepted, was the way of the world and recognising the significance of the murder and its importance to the police at least gave Donnelly a starting point in his search for bargaining power. For he had no intention of remaining a squad target for a moment longer than was absolutely necessary. And he was astute enough to understand that with the right commodity on offer, you could bargain your way out of anything.

So by flattery and subtle questioning he proceeded to pick Vic Hardwick's brain clean on the subject of the Eastgate murder.

'All right,' Donnelly said at last, 'let's see if I've got it straight. The kid's body's found in the boot of an old banger which belongs to this guy Murphy who's a dead ringer for the job only you can't pin it on him because he's got a cast iron alibi backed up by a bunch of upright citizens. So now you're all beating around the undergrowth looking for some other likely candidate. Is that about the strength of it, Vic?'

'I don't know why you're so interested in this case,' Hardwick replied morosely, 'Not now you're a big deal squad target who can't even play fair with his own brother-in-law.'

'Just humour me Vic, OK?' said Donnelly easily. 'Did I get it about right?'

'I suppose so.'

'This alibi,' Donnelly mused, 'can you get me a look at the statements?'

'Well, I don't know about that,' Hardwick began to protest, 'that's official business and besides. . . .'

'Victor, this is a family thing, would I ask you otherwise? Besides you're an important man, *the* crime intelligence specialist. Don't sell yourself short Vic.'

'What if I could get 'em,' Hardwick scowled miserably, and Donnelly eased himself back in his chair.

'Wouldn't you like things back the way they were Vic, like the good old days?'

'Yes but . . . .'

'Trust me Vic. . OK? Get me those statements and I'll see what I can do.' Donnelly reached for the cabinet beside his desk. 'Now how about a drink to calm the old nerves?'

Hardwick heaved himself to his feet. 'No thanks,' he turned the offer down emphatically. 'I've been here too long already. Associating with a squad target! Jesus, they could boil me in oil for that.'

Donnelly shrugged. 'It'll be all right Vic, you'll see,' he said persuasively. 'Just get me a shufti at those statements, OK?'

'I can't bring 'em here,' Hardwick protested and Donnelly laughed at his pained expression.

'Why not? You're always down here Vic. Break the pattern and you'll be next on the surveillance.'

An involuntary groan escaped Hardwick's lips as he imagined the squad staking out the split level bungalow which was his wife's pride and joy. Mavis would crucify him.

'Just get the statements,' Donnelly urged, patting his arm in a gesture of brotherly affection, 'and trust me Vic, OK?'

* * *

It was, Hardwick discovered, surprisingly easy. He borrowed the closely typed statement sheets from the incident room on the pretext of checking with his MO index, ran photocopies and returned the originals before anybody could ask awkward questions. The following day he was back at his brother-in-law's yard sitting across the desk and gnawing his knuckles anxiously as he watched Donnelly read through the copies, hoping for a change of expression which would indicate a ray of hope. He had slept badly the night before, plagued by nightmares of vultures circling as he staggered exhausted across an endless desert. Donnelly read in silence, absorbing the stilted prose, taking particular interest in the alibi which he re-read several times.

'These people,' he broke the deep silence finally, 'they've got damned good memories.'

'Unshakable,' the detective replied gloomily. 'He couldn't have planned it better if he'd wanted to. They all tell the same story and if you're thinking of collusion, forget it. They've all been checked out.'

Donnelly smiled. 'But if one cracks then they all go out the window?'

'They won't,' Hardwick replied. 'There's enough witnesses there to sink a battleship. That's the best alibi I ever saw. Hotel guests, staff, people he never even knew. It's fireproof.'

'This one,' Donnelly said, alighting on one of the names. 'This guy George Bodkins, what d'you know about him?'

Hardwick frowned, dredging his memory. 'Him . . . oh yeah,' he replied, 'He's the garage owner with the XJ6. Was stopping over on a business trip.'

'Didn't know Murphy from Adam either,' Donnelly mused.

'That's right,' Hardwick agreed. 'How'd he put it? Oh yeah, – just helping out a fellow traveller and doing his public duty. That's what he said.'

Donnelly's smiled widened. 'Nice touch,' he said.

* * *

When Hardwick had gone Alex Donnelly called in two of his biggest ugliest yard hands and dispatched them to Bodkins' garage with an invitation the man couldn't refuse unless he fancied a length of lead pipe bent over his cranium. They returned with a pasty faced man who sported a Zapata moustache and seemed to be having trouble with his breathing.

'Hello Odds,' Donnelly greeted him. 'Long time no see.' He rose, smoothing down the jacket of his pinstripe suit. 'Good of you to come at such short notice.'

Bodkins gasped for air like a stranded fish, breath whistling from his lungs. His voice was a nasal whine. 'I thought you and me was mates Alex, you didn't have to go and set these gorillas to work me over – busted half me ribs.'

'Tried to leg it out the window gaffer,' explained the larger of the two messengers. 'Got so excited we had to give him a tap.'

'All right lads,' Donnelly told the pair, 'just wait outside a minutes while I talk to Mr Bodkins here.'

When they were alone Donnelly poured his guest a drink. 'What I want you to understand Odds,' he said apologetically as he handed him a generous tumbler of whiskey, 'is there's nothing personal in this whatsoever. 'It's pure business.'

'What'd I do?' Bodkins yelped, gulping at the Scotch in the hope of fortifying himself.

'It's a long story,' Donnelly told him in his quiet courteous manner, 'but let's put it this way, you're a good careful villain Odds, I've got to give you that. You've got a nice thriving little firm ringing bent motors and shipping 'em out without the law even getting a sniff, a nice sensible living with plenty of prospects.' Donnelly's eyes grew cold. 'So why'd you have to go and spoil it all by getting mixed up with a toe rag like this Murphy character?'

Bodkins' eyes widened, but he still tried to brazen it out. 'I don't know what you mean Alex.'

'What I mean,' Donnelly explained patiently, 'is you fitted this scum up with an alibi.'

'Hey Alex,' Bodkins cried. 'What would I do a thing like that for?'

'And the trouble is,' Donnelly went on, ignoring the protestation, 'owing to certain circumstances affecting myself and my associates, I'm going to have to get you to throw your friend Murphy to the wolves.'

'For God's sake Alex,' Bodkins blurted, his face ashen, 'it wasn't my idea. I just went along with it. Jesus if I'd known it was going to cause you problems Alex I'd have told 'em to shove it, on my baby's eyes I would.'

A faint regretful smile touched Donnelly's lips. 'No sense in getting all worked up Odds,' he said, 'as I explained, this is purely business. We've always got on well in the past, you stick to your side of the fence and I stick to mine, but you see it finally comes down to a question of priorities.'

'What d'you want me to do Alex,' Bodkins asked desperately, 'anything you want, just name it.'

Donnelly examined his finger nails. 'I want you to dump Murphy. Make a new statement to the police. Say you were mistaken. An honest mistake, must've been someone else. I'll take care of the arrangements.'

'Anything you say Alex,' Bodkins gabbled. 'You're the boss – anything you say. . . .'

'You're still missing the point,' Donnelly spoke quietly, polishing his nails on his sleeve and then inspecting the shine, 'I'm going to have to make an example of you Odds so that all those cronies of yours get the message. But I want you to believe me when I tell you there's absolutely nothing personal in this at all. You've got to look on it as a business transaction, a little sacrifice in the name of goodwill.'

Bodkins yelped in fright as Donnelly recalled his henchmen and they dragged the man squealing and struggling out into the yard and strapped him into the driving seat of his XJ6.

The Jaguar was a pale beige, its lovingly Simonized flanks gleaming like gold; the upholstery was soft brown hide. It sat there sleek and contented in sharp contrast to the dirty yellow

Hy-Mac yard crane which loomed over it, its four great rusty claws poised over the roof. At a sign from Donnelly, the talons swooped down and seized the car, rocked it on its suspension then swung it effortlessly into the air, glass and paint flakes showered down as the hydraulic grab bit into the roof. Roaring and belching smoke from its sooty exhaust stack, the Hy-Mac jiggled the car in mid air, then crashed it to the ground. A hub cap spun off and went tinkling across the yard. Inside the Jaguar, Bodkins was screaming in terror as the crane heaved the car into the air again, shaking it like a terrier worrying a bone. This time pieces of metal fell off before the crane let go and the Jaguar crashed back to the ground. A wheel came away and bounced into the scrap pile.

At Donnelly's signal the process was repeated several times until, bent and buckled, the XJ6 looked very sorry for itself and from inside the wrecked car Bodkins could be heard wailing hysterically. After a moment Donnelly gave the instruction for the claws to relax their grip, setting the car down for the last time with a shriek of tortured metal. Odds Bodkins had screamed himself hoarse as battered and misshapen the once sleek epitome of automotive design had been effortlessly reduced to scrap. He was gibbering like an idiot when they hauled him out of the wreck and deposited him at Donnelly's feet. Spittle drooled from his lips and his eyes swivelled in his head as he scrabbled about in the dirt and ended up clinging to Donnelly's leg.

'No hard feelings Odds,' Donnelly told him solicitously, 'Oh and I hope this Jag of yours is still under warranty, otherwise I think you just lost your no-claims bonus.'

* * *

Some time later Dennis Jewel, the Crime Squad DCI looked in on his friend Brian Webber at the S Division CID.

'See you cleared that Eastgate job then Brian,' Jewel remarked admiringly.

'Not so loud Dennis,' Webber protested, clutching his head, He had not yet recovered from the party they had thrown to celebrate the murder arrest in time honoured tradition. He had awful memories of DCs being sick in the alley adjoining the pub, another attempting to drunkenly seduce a barmaid fell down the cellar steps and broke his leg. And usually staid DS danced a jig on a table wearing only his underpants and then led the assembly in community hymn singing before collapsing into a paralytic stupor. Webber shuddered at the memory.

'Good bit of work that,' Jewel congratulated him without moderating his voice. 'Commendations all round so I heard. What happened Brian, some sharp D get lucky?'

Webber sighed. 'Damnedest thing Dennis,' he said, 'Chummy's alibi just blew up in his face. Just evaporated.'

'Get away.'

'He had all those witnesses in his pocket. You know what he was up to? He'd been putting on live porno shows, all sorts of kinky stuff at that hotel. They were all his regulars and they were terrified if they didn't play along with him he'd mark all their cards, wreck their marriages, and they'd be out of the Rotary club. While they were getting a cheap thrill he was out knocking off this kid. Sadistic bastard, thought he was fireproof.'

'Nice one,' Jewel said admiringly. 'Who pulled the rug out from under?'

Webber winced at the pain behind his eyes. 'That old has-been Vic Hardwick, would you believe,' he replied. 'Been out to grass in crime intelligence longer than I can remember, then bang, he's got this one sewn up and covered himself in glory.'

'Luck of the draw probably,' Jewel said. 'What'd old Vic do, rub his lamp three times and get himself a genie?'

'Something like that,' Webber agreed. 'He'd got a bloody good informant that's for sure, some guy he'd been cultivating for years, got a nice citizen's commendation from the chief for his public spirited co-operation.'

'Wouldn't be some superstar called Alex Donnelly would it?'

'Yeah – that's right,' Webber said with some surprise.

'How'd you know that Dennis?'

Jewel scratched his ear. 'That explained it,' he said, 'I got a curt note from upstairs about him. We'd got him marked as a Zatopek target.'

'What?'

'Hmm – just one of those things.'

'What'd you do?'

'Oh we dropped him like a hot brick. How'd you like to explain away a squad target who just cleared a murder with a chief's commendation in his pocket to prove it.'

'I wouldn't.'

'Neither would I,' Jewel said. 'I had his stuff yanked out of the index and through the shredder so fast you wouldn't have known he existed.'

'Self preservation,' Weber nodded.

'That's the name of the game,' Jewel grinned and looked at his watch. 'Well they're open Brian, how about a jar? Hair of the dog.'

Webber lowered his head onto his hands. 'Go away Dennis,' he retorted, steadying his brow and waiting for the spasm of nausea to pass.

Fifteen The Inspection

THE mess dinner at the end of the HMI's annual inspection was, as tradition dictated, a formal affair. The mess silver was displayed and proper etiquette scrupulously observed. Only the select few had been invited, for Henry Grey had personally supervised the guest list. Resplendent in his immaculately tailored mess kit, the deputy chief surveyed the gathering around the table with satisfaction, well scrubbed faces aglow in the soft flickering light from the candlebra. Only one small doubt disturbed him as his gaze alighted on a small clique of detectives at the far end of the table. He had been prevailed upon, against his better judgement, to include a CID contingent to celebrate the solving of the Eastgate murder. As they took their places he regarded them with a jaundiced eye; at least they'd had the common decency to wear dinner jackers for the occasion.

It had been a bad day Grey reflected as Sir Ralph Hawk said Grace. A day which had begun with a unnerving encounter with Maxwell Cheep the S Divisional commander, whose desperate requests for an audience, the deputy chief could no longer ignore.

Cheep had stumbled into the office, haggard and drawn and without hesitation, had begun to plead for a transfer from S Division.

'But what's happend?' Grey wanted to know. 'This was your big chance, everybody expected great things from you.'

'They've got at me,' Cheep exclaimed, a nervous tic jigging the left side of his face.

'They – who're they?' Grey demanded.

'Them – THEM,' Cheep's eyes rolled and his face contorted in an effort to impress his predicament upon the deputy.

'Them?' Grey echoed, feeling both foolish and embarrassed at the same time.

'You don't know them sir,' Cheep shuddered at the thought, 'I can't take it any longer.'

'Pull yourself together man' commanded the deputy, but

I DON'T UNDERSTAND IT MAX, WE ZOOMED YOU INTO FULL EXPOSURE, YOU WERE RIGHT IN FOCUS. GET YOUR TRANSFER DOWN IN BLACK AND WHITE AND WE WILL SEE WHAT DEVELOPS.
P.C.
N. BUTT

Cheep threw himself forward and clutched the edge of the desk. 'Sir – I implore you – get me out of that place.'

Grey recoiled in horror. He thought for a moment that Cheep was going to fling himself at his feet. 'I'll talk to personnel,' he promised weakly and Cheep beside himself with gratitude, clutched his hand and refused to let go for several minutes.

Yes, that unfortunate episode had unnerved Grey for the rest of the day. Even his paperwork seemed to be dogged by some awful spectre of S Division. There was a report on a PC named Nigel Butt saying that he had been admitted to a psychiatric hospital with an acute mental disorder and that a medical discharge from the force was recommended. Grey signed the document with the same foreboding with which he had propelled the simpering Cheep from his office. What with that and the crime squad complaining they weren't getting enough co-operation on Zatopek, and the chief delegating all the dirty jobs, Grey felt sorely used by the end of the day. Now in the tranquil surroundings of the mess, he yearned for nothing more than a little civilised company. He echoed the sentiments of Sir Ralph Hawk who gave thanks for good fellowship and good food and then took his seat at Grey's right hand. White gloved cadets served the soup.

'Consider the Jock-strap Act of 1984,' said Sir Ralph, apropos of nothing, and as usual Henry Grey was immediately dismayed at his own inadequacy in the face of the HMI's conversational gambit. 'A trifle Orwellian perhaps,' went on Sir Ralph, 'But nontheless valid, eh Henry.'

The best Grey could offer was an attentive ear. He smiled and nodded and busied himself with his soup.

'Think about it for a moment Henry,' said the HMI. 'Here we have a new law enacted by a benign Parliament to improve the posture of the adult male. Enter the police officer empowered under the new regulation to stop and question on suspicion.' The HMI finished his soup and a white gloved hand whisked the plate away. 'Excuse me, sir,' he continued, impersonating the hypothetical officer, 'I've followed you for one tenth of a mile and I have reason to believe having observed your gait that you are in contravention of the athletic supporter and correct posture act. Would you mind dropping your trousers so that I can verify my suspicions.' The HMI returned to his own voice. 'Naturally the citizen refuses to comply in no uncertain terms and ends up in the pokey for the night and court the following morning. Fifty pounds fine or three months on summary conviction, just because he preferred to dangle.'

Henry Grey felt it safe to laugh. 'Very good Sir Ralph, very droll.'

'It makes my point though Henry,' the HMI told him. 'There's just too much of it about.'

'Jock straps Sir Ralph?' Grey asked with a puzzled frown.

'The criminal law,' rebuked the HMI.

'Ah I see.' They were halfway through the escalope of veal and Grey caught the eye of the wine waiter and beckoned him across. 'A little more wine Sir Ralph?' As the glasses were topped up, Grey took the opportunity of glowering in the direction of the CID party who were already on their third bottle.

'The point I'm making, whimsically perhaps,' said Sir Ralph breezily, 'is that too many politicians believe they can regulate the entire human condition simply by passing laws. Why – there's so much criminal law about, Henry, that it we tried to enforce it all we'd be buried under the avalanche.

'Oh I take your point Sir Ralph,' said Grey, slightly preoccupied with an elaborate mime to indicate that the debris of the main course should be cleared away. The meal was proceeding with military precision.

Over the raspberry water ice, the HMI turned to a more tangible topic. The Eastgate murder.

'What was the girl's name Henry?' he asked.

'Which girl?'

'The one who was murdered.'

Grey hadn't the slightest idea. Throughout the investigation it hadn't occurred to him to inquire the girl's name. She was always referred to as 'the victim'. Now that the file had been completed and parcelled off to the Director of Public

Prosecutions, the girl's identity was of no particular interest. After all the offender – his name too escaped him – was before the court. Grey scribbled a note on his place card and instructed one of the cadets to pass it discreetly to the most senior of the CID group. Detectives took an interest in things like names. But the CID contingent must have thought it was a joke for the arrival of the note brought a ripple of laughter and glances in his direction, but no response. The Deputy fumed in silence and fortunately, the HMI didn't pursue the point.

'I thought that TV programme was excellent.'

'Which one was that Sir Ralph?' Grey asked automatically, still occupied with his meaningful glowering.

'*Close Up*. You know the trick with that programme is the realism they manage to portray. The real nitty-gritty. Wonderful piece on public co-operation. Made a few other forces sit up and take notice.'

'We were very pleased,' said Grey. The port had circulated several times and now seemed stalled with the CID group. One of the detectives guffawed too loudly for Grey's liking. Cheese and biscuits came and went. Coffee was poured and Grey nibbled an After-Eight.

'Of course you've got some really bright young men,' the HMI observed. 'Take young Lawson for example,' he'll go a long way, make my words.'

'Do you think so Sir Ralph?' Grey was less than enthusiastic as he picked out the ACC in the candlelight massaging his crew cut with the flat of his hand, oblivious of the conversation washing around him.

'Oh definitely,' Sir Ralph told him. 'He's getting quite a reputation for original thought. They think very highly of him in the Home Office. Why that presentation he gave at the College on the approach to police practice in a weightless environment was the most original thing they'd ever heard. You watch that boy Henry – he's going places.'

The enormity of the idea was too much for Henry Grey to grasp. He masked his confusion by passing the port once more. Then it was time for the loyal toast. The detectives were talking loudly now, faces flushed, bow ties askew.

After the toasts, Sir Ralph Hawk rose to his feet, swaying slightly as Grey rapped the miniature gavel in the time honoured signal for a respectful silence.

'Mister President,' Sir Ralph addressed Grey formally in his capacity as President of the Mess and then turned to the gathering: 'Gentlemen. It is always a pleasure to escape from the cloistered world of the Home Office to visit a force with such fine traditions as yours. Without men like you – men of vision, men of intellect and determination in the face of adversity, the police service of this country would be a mere shadow. Progress – that must be our watchword. I commend to your progress – with a human face.' The HMI paused for effect, weaving slightly and then plunged on: 'The murder at Eastgate was a classic example of police tenacity, investigative skills and service to the community. A fine piece of work, and you can rest assured that I will be putting a word in on your behalf. . . .'

'Where?' shouted one of the detectives through a haze of port fumes, 'Where?'

The dastardly breach of etiquette brought a stunned silence for half a moment as Sir Ralph Hawk allowed his eyes to rise slowly towards the ceiling, 'Where it counts,' he replied, 'where it counts.'